SECO
SPACE

RACHEL AUKES

WAYPOINT BOOKS

SECONDHAND SPACEMAN SERIES

WAYPOINT BOOKS

SECONDHAND SPACEMAN
Secondhand Spaceman Series, Book 1

Edited by Diane Bryant

Ebook ASIN: B0CLQNDZ9B
Print ISBN: 978-1-956120-05-9

———

Sign up for Rachel's newsletter to be the first to hear about
new releases and upcoming projects: www.rachelaukes.
com/join

For Brian, always.

CONTENTS

YOUR GUIDE TO BEING AN INTERGALACTIC RECLAMATION AGENT

WELCOME, *new intergalactic reclamation agent!*

By signing a work contract with Starshine Seizure Specialists (**SSS**), you have tenured yourself to a universally renowned repossession agency to reclaim, repossess, and retrieve any and all items required to satisfy customers' tickets. Instructions and logistics are included with every reclamation ticket.

Here are a few items to keep in mind:

1. If you fail to complete an assigned reclamation ticket, you may be penalized with additional years added to your work contract.
2. If you fail to follow the instructions detailed in a reclamation ticket, you may not be paid for that ticket and you may be penalized with additional years added to your work contract.
3. You represent Starshine Seizure Specialists at all times. That means no murdering, pillaging, or associating with scum; or else you

may be penalized with additional years added to your work contract.

4. You are required to own and maintain your transport. The company is not liable for damage or breakage of any assets used in pursuit of a ticket. The company will not provide you with a transport. Without a transport, you will not be able to complete a reclamation ticket (Refer to Item 1).

5. And never, ever skip out on your work contract with SSS. Your life and assets are forfeited should you do so.

Refer to your contract for required liability disclaimers. Mistakes could lead to space disease, dismemberment, your body being taken over by parasites, death, violations issued by GOD, and— most importantly—reflect poorly on Starshine Seizure Specialists.

Best wishes in surviving your contract. Now, get to work.*

*Take pride in being a SSS reclamation agent. Customers choose Starshine Seizure Specialists because we have the highest success rate of all repossession companies in the galaxy. Customers know our agents live (and die) by our motto, *"We cover the Milky Way so you don't have to."*

1 / ALIENS ARE REAL (AND THEY SUCK)

A LOT of great stories begin with Boy meets Girl. Mine's no different except right after Boy met Girl, things turned *weird*.

I'd been minding my own business, running to class (I was late again, but in my defense, I'd been in the middle of a most excellent video game) when she slammed into me from behind. I barely kept myself from face-planting on the sidewalk.

"Oh, I'm *so* sorry," a sweet, feminine voice said.

I spun to chew her out; I gaped instead. This redhead wore faded jeans and a white low-cut V-neck shirt that accentuated curves I didn't think existed outside the pages of a *Playboy* magazine.

She personified *lusciousness*.

"S'okay," I managed to get out, which was impressive considering that my brain had fully disconnected from my body. In my defense, her V-neck was *really* low-cut.

She bent to pick up the books she'd dropped, revealing a butterfly tattoo on her lower back. I admired the artwork, or something like that.

"Here, allow me." I rushed to pick up her books and noticed an Advanced Calculus textbook. Gorgeous and smart, and *way* out of my league.

She smiled as she tucked them under her arm. "Thank you, Frank."

The campus bells rang at the top of the hour. Class had just started, which meant it was a galactic inevitability that my grade just dropped to a C for recurring tardiness. Not that grades *really* matter when you're going to be a truck driver, but still, I have *some* ambition.

I frowned. "Wait a second. You know me?"

"Of course. You're the reason I'm here."

She grabbed my hand. Her skin was surprisingly cold to the touch and really... *squishy*. A jolt of electric lava shot from her palm and through me, followed by a numbing blackness that drowned me.

I woke to a blinding light and the pungent stink of sweaty gym socks. The gray floor under me looked like it'd started out as white a long time ago. My head throbbed, and I brought my hand up to find a goose egg on my forehead. "Ow."

I noticed my hand hurt, too, and I found three raised red dots on my palm. I adjusted my glasses, but they were dirty. I tried to clean them on my shirt but probably just wound up rearranging the dirt. When I slid them back on, I found the hot girl from campus standing in front of me.

"Your head hurts because you hit it on the

sidewalk. That's not my fault. Maybe next time you'll pass out on the grass," she sneered.

Why were hot girls always so mean?

"What hap..." I trailed off as my memories returned. I kicked away, scurrying until my back was pressed against a wall. I pointed at her. "*You*... what'd you do to me?"

"Transporting you in your unconscious form was the most efficient way to transport you. It's a well-known fact that your kind isn't known for its intelligence, and I didn't want to spend time tending to your questions."

"Not *all* guys are idiots, you know." I shoved to my feet, scanning the big gray, cube-shaped room. The walls were the same dirty color as the floor and covered in scuffs and stains. There didn't seem to be a door, let alone windows. "I can't believe it! You've *kidnapped* me.! The hottest girl I've ever seen, and she kidnaps me! Inconceivable!"

"I most certainly did not kidnap you. On the contrary, I've already filed all the necessary revised forms to onboard you. I was fortunate to have found you. New paperwork takes forever to process right now, what with the Rifugellian protests and all."

I started to feel utterly trapped. "Where am I? Why am I here? What are you going to do to me?"

"I can answer all your questions with a single statement: you're here because you're going to work for me," she said.

"Thanks but no thanks. I'll pass. Let me out of here now, and I won't press charges. People are going to come looking for me." My stupid voice crackled with nervousness.

She chuckled, and the sound was more sinister than pleasant. "We both know that no one's going to come looking for you, Frank Woods, son of Caleb Woods. You have no family, and your only friend, at this very moment, is in bed, fornicating with your girlfriend."

"Ex-girlfriend, and ex-friend." At least as of a whole three hours ago. My eyes narrowed. "Ah, I get it. You're one of Clarissa's friends, aren't you? Just because I dumped her, she's decided to do some sort of messed up, psycho revenge thing, hasn't she?"

"I've never been in contact with your girlfriend."

"*Ex*-girlfriend." I reiterated. "And tell Clarissa she's gone way too far this time. Whatever *this* is." I gestured around me. "It ain't funny."

She eyed me for a moment. "I hope I didn't fly all the way out here, in the middle of nowhere, to pick up a defective."

"You flew to Nebraska just for *me?*"

"Of course," she replied, the annoyance transparent in her voice. "Why else would you be on my ship right now?"

"Ship? Wait, I thought you said you flew here. Why are we on a boat?"

"Wrong kind of ship, you bonehead."

"Hey, sticks and stones may break my bones, but words will never hurt me," I sang.

"You're on my *space*ship."

I chortled. "Sure thing. Ha ha—holy crap!"

The room had morphed from a small, whitish

room to a larger, whitish room. In the expanded space, screens covered one wall, and cabling ran along all corners and edges. A cylindrical tube sat against another wall. Round windows now appeared on every wall, the floor, and even ceiling. None of the windows were of the same size, which made them look like something Alice would find in Wonderland.

It was dark outside, but I'd been on my way to my ten AM class. Even worse, it seemed *too* dark outside despite the stars twinkling brighter than I'd ever seen them. There were no streetlights, which could only mean I was no longer near campus. I hustled to the nearest window, pressing my hands and nose against the glass. At first, it was too dark to make out anything, but as my eyes adjusted, I could see something in the distance. I squinted. It was round and mostly dark, but a section was kind of, sort of lit up. It took a moment for my brain to point out that the shape reminded me of Australia.

I stumbled backward and pointed. "That's—that's—that's—"

"Earth?" she answered for me.

I nodded robotically.

"As I told you before, you're on my ship."

"I thought you were lying."

"A Zuddlian never lies... unless there's a profit in it, of course," she replied indignantly. She crossed her arms over her chest, and even undergoing a current bout of insanity, I glanced at her cleavage.

"This can't be a spaceship," I said, realizing that I sounded more whiny than confident. "Because if it was, that means I've lost my freaking mind. Wait, am I hallucinating? You didn't just knock me out; you gave me some kind of hallucinogenic drugs, too, didn't you? What'd you give me? LSD? PCP? Ecstasy? Something else?"

She sighed. "You're aboard my ship; whether or not you're insane is an entirely separate issue. Though, I certainly hope you're not insane since you're legally obligated to work for me," she said, totally serious. "I suppose an introduction is in order. My name's Totty. I'm a managing director of Starshine Seizure Specialists, and you're on my ship, *Totty*."

I cocked my head. "Wait. Your name's Totty, and your ship's name's *Totty*?"

She nodded. "Yes."

"You named your ship after you?"

"What's wrong with that?"

I shrugged. "Just seems a bit pretentious, don't you think?"

"It's my ship, and *Totty* is an excellent name. And since my race is vastly superior to yours, I have every right to be pretentious."

I cocked my head. "You're saying you're not... like me?"

She stared at me drily. "I'm going to deactivate the hologram. Try not to panic or wet yourself."

"What ho—holy crap!" I jumped back as the redheaded woman before me morphed into a purple jellybean about two feet tall. She—*it*—had two big black eyes and weird little feet with overly long toes. The creature would've been cute if it wasn't covered in warts. I kept as much distance between us as possible. This acid trip had just taken a turn from weird to *super* weird. "Who, no, WHAT the hell are you?"

"I told you. I'm a Zuddlian, but more importantly, I am the holder of your work contract. That makes me your employer, and I must say, thus far, I'm not impressed by the amount of respect you show your superiors, or lack thereof." Her voice had morphed into a squeaky voice that didn't sound quite human, more like someone after sucking a helium balloon. Her words also seemed to come from the air itself, as the creature had no mouth.

My jaw hung slack as I stared at the *thing* before me.

"You're not going into cardiac arrest, are you?" Totty asked.

I continued to stare.

"Are you going into a catatonic state, maybe?"

She sighed. "You see? That's why I used the hologram. A lesser being's first encounter with a superior race can be a bit discombobulating."

I blinked. She didn't look superior. She looked like the *Creature from the Black Lagoon* pooped a giant purple turd with little turds for its toes and feet.

She cocked her head. "Did your mind break? Say something."

"I'm talking to a jellybean."

"And there I was, hoping you weren't a complete idiot like your father," Totty said.

"Wait, what?" I jerked. "What about my father?"

"Who do you think signed the work contract indenturing you to Starshine Seizure Specialists?"

2 / EVERYTHING REALLY IS AS BAD AS IT SEEMS

"You've got the wrong guy," I said. "I don't even have a father."

"Oh? Let me guess, you were immaculately conceived, the old virgin birth story, eh? Oddly, every race has one of them," Totty said wryly.

"What? No. I mean, I have a biological father, duh, but the dude ran off on Mom and me right after I turned four. Dude's a deadbeat dad." I shrugged. "I don't even remember him. So if he owes you something, trust me, you're not going to get anything from me."

"That doesn't matter. Biological links are all that matter based on the tenure contract he signed," the alien said. "You were provided a copy of the contract. Did you not read it?"

I racked my brain for memories of such a contract. "I don't know what you're talking about."

"Your ineptitude is not my problem. A contract's a contract, and your father signed one."

If there were used car salesmen in space, I had a feeling Totty was one of them. She didn't exactly come across as honest. "And what *exactly* did he sign?"

"He agreed to work for Sunshine Seizure Specialists—my company—for a specified length of time in exchange for full ownership of his own ship."

"Oh, like a person can sign up for space travel, just like that," I said sarcastically. "Like, since humans made it to the moon, they can now sign up for their own spaceships." I raised my hand. "I'll take one spaceship, hold the under-coating."

"No one can simply *sign* up. You—especially a Terran—must be vetted. Your father happened to come across one of my reclamation agents who was on your planet, recovering stolen property. The laws are quite explicit about non-interstellar races such as yours: they cannot interact with interstellar races. Yes, *technically,* Terrans are interstellar since examples of your technology have traveled beyond your star system. However, per the letter of universal law, Terrans aren't considered interstellar. Therefore, I proposed a quite generous offer to your father: he could work for me."

"Or?"

"Or?" she echoed, confused.

"He could work for you or what? You make it sound like it was an ultimatum," I said.

"Oh, yes. He could work for me, or he'd be exterminated, of course. Clearly, you can't have a non-interstellar race learn about interstellar races and then be left to their own devices. Chaos would ensue. If there's one thing I'm most certainly not, that's a lawbreaker," Totty replied.

I put as much space between me and the alien as I could. This was the most real nightmare

I'd ever had. I voiced my question softly, "So his choice was to work for you or die?"

"Bluntly stated, but yes."

I swallowed dread. "That's not a choice; that's coercion."

"You make it sound harsh."

"That's because it is harsh!"

"Your father was grateful to have been given a choice, and he wisely chose to work for me. He signed a standard tenured work contract. See," she said as she turned to a screen that displayed a page of gibberish, weird curvy symbols filled the screen with a scrawled signature, Caleb Woods, at the bottom.

I ignored the screen. "Where is he? I want to talk to him."

"You can't. He's dead," she answered.

I stood there, feeling an odd sense of loss for someone I didn't even remember. But even more than loss, I felt fear. "You killed him."

"Of course not. He made me money, and now it's your turn. His contract stipulated that, upon his death, his next living heir would assume his responsibility and complete the time remaining on the contract. That's *you*. Hence, that is why I had to travel four systems—out of my way, mind you—to collect you."

I shook my head. "I can't believe a guy would sign away his only kid. No way."

"Being a Terran, he probably didn't even read the fine print. Even if he had, he probably assumed he wouldn't die before his contract obligations had been fulfilled. I don't imagine he intended his guts to be a host for seven hundred Gee eggs."

I recoiled. "He was implanted with alien babies, like on *Alien*?"

"I'm not familiar with the particular alien of which you're talking about, but yes, he was implanted with alien offspring. When they hatched, they had to break free of their nest. A Gee tried to plant its eggs in me once, but my skin is too tough for them. Disgusting little creatures," Totty said.

I stared blankly. I'd often wished for my dad to suffer after what he'd put my mom and me through, like him stuck in prison or having to work in a certain superstore's warehouse. But going out *Alien*-style? Never saw that one coming.

"What matters is that the contract now passes on to you. You are legally bound to fulfill your father's obligations," Totty said.

I shook my head. "No way, no how. That's not how contracts work. I didn't sign nothing." Technically, I'd signed three contracts before: one for my phone, one for a credit card, and one for my apartment lease; and none involved forced slavery.

"My grasp of your language is better than yours, and I'm not a native speaker."

I ignored her comment. "There's no way a contract can be enforced if I didn't sign it."

"Oh, you're an expert on universal law now, Terran?"

"*Dick*," I muttered under my breath before saying louder, "I want to go home. Take me home right now."

Totty gestured with one of her bulbous toes. "The door's right there."

I eyed the door, gritted my teeth, and turned

back to the alien. "No. You gotta take me home. You kidnapped me; you take me back to campus, exactly where you drugged me."

"I have no desire to return to that bug-infested dust bowl you call a home world. I'm a generous soul, and I'm offering you the same deal I proposed to your father. You can walk out the door behind you or sign the contract. There is no third option."

We held a staring contest for many, *many* long seconds, but Totty never blinked. Looking back, I realized she doesn't even have eyelids. I might've stood my ground a bit longer if I'd known. But who am I kidding? Life had never gone my way—I'd long since gotten used to that and kind of anticipated being given a choice that was somewhere between an asteroid and a hard place.

"How much time is left on his contract?" I asked finally, resignedly.

She waddled over to the contract on the screen. The gibberish moved on the screen even though she had no hands to move anything. "Slightly over three hundred and sixty-two years."

"Say what?!"

"Oh, that's in universal standard time. In Earth standard time, it's, let's see, yes, it's only sixty-eight of your years, plus four months and two weeks...give or take a few seconds."

My shock didn't ebb at the new number. "Are you nuts? I'm nineteen. In sixty-eight years, I'd be eighty-seven. That's like *ancient* in human years! Seriously, I'd probably be in a wheelchair by then, probably even wearing diapers. I'll die up here."

"In all likelihood, yes, but hopefully not before you fulfill your contract. I want a full return on my investment."

At the idea of death, terror decided to take over right then. I sprinted to each window, searching for a way out, but each window showed only more black space outside. I was panting, on the verge of hyperventilating, as I continued to run around the shoebox-shaped room. I must've checked each window at least three times, including the windows in the floor and ceiling. I made my way to the screens, but there were no keyboards—no inputs of any kind—the glass didn't even respond when I ran my fingers across it.

"Are you finished? You're running around like a rabid Anzu," Totty said.

I scowled at the purple jellybean before making one more round through the claustrophobic ship, stopping at the hatch. If I tried to escape, I'd die from exposure in under two agonizing minutes. Of course, that was assuming everything I was seeing was real—I wasn't convinced it was. Shoot, for all I knew, this was some weird reality TV show, and if I opened the hatch, I might see a camera crew on the other side.

I grabbed the handle.

"I'd advise against that. It's terribly chilly outside."

I lifted the handle. It was surprisingly easy.

"I can withstand the cold vacuum of space. You can't," Totty said. It almost sounded like a challenge.

Pulling open the door was harder. I gave it a good yank, and it opened inward. My ears popped, and my glasses frosted over in an instant. A breeze pressed at my back, as though encouraging me to step outside. My eyes felt like they were bulging. I tried to breathe, but there wasn't enough air; as if I was somewhere really high up, like on Mount Everest. But the worst part about standing in that doorway was the frigid cold. Nothing I'd ever felt before came close to this deep-freeze, and I'd experienced a lifetime of Nebraska winters. It was so cold that I stared in shock for a second before slamming the door closed and collapsing to the floor.

Of all the sensations I'd felt since coming awake—from seeing and hearing a weird little alien to seeing a spaceship (which was much more boring-looking than I'd expected a spaceship to look like)—feeling the brutal temperature and the sensation of a vacuum is what convinced me: this was no hallucination. I wasn't having some weird, drugged-up mind trip. How it was real was *way* beyond my comprehension, but I knew deep down, as deep down as the new chill in my bones, that Totty wasn't lying.

I really had been kidnapped by an alien and was in space aboard her ship.

"Did that make you feel better?" she asked before complaining, "It's going to take an hour to warm it back up in here."

I ignored her, instead choosing to stare blankly out a window as my glasses slowly defrosted. Earth was now just a tiny blue dot in the distance. I could empathize with lab rats—I now knew exactly how they felt. I existed at the whim of a purple mad scientist.

I was Totty's rat.

Biting back the urge to scream, I gave Totty a grim look. "What do I have to do?"

She grinned, if you can imagine an alien with no mouth making that sort of expression, and it was a very ugly, very chilling thing.

3 / ALWAYS READ THE SMALL PRINT

"Sign on the dotted line, and you'll be the newest contractor of Starshine Seizure Specialists. That's triple-S for short," Totty said.

I squinted at the screen of gibberish. "I can't read it."

"Oh, I forgot you don't have a translator. Not that I'd expect a Terran to understand a universal tenured work contract, anyway." She didn't move, but something happened because the gibberish morphed into English.

"How'd you do that, change the screen like that without touching anything?" How did she do anything without hands, for that matter? How'd she wipe her butt? Did she even have a butt? I realized I didn't want to know. I adjusted my glasses and focused on the screen.

"I come from a highly advanced race. Once we developed telekinesis, we evolved into not requiring hands, not to mention arms," she answered.

"Ah, so, magic," I said.

"How your race has survived as long as it has is beyond me," she said. "Now, sign the contract so I can get you on your way. I've already had you on my ship over a day longer than I prefer. You've stunk up the place with your Terran breath."

I stiffened. "I've been here over a day already?"

"A day in universal standard time. Again. For your slow-firing brain, that means you've been on my ship for over two Earth hours. You know, you need to quit using Earth standard time and soon. It annoys me."

"I'm glad it annoys you," I muttered before turning back to the screen.

I tried to comprehend two paragraphs—each covering a full screen—before my eyes crossed. No wonder my dad had skimmed over the fine print. I thought contracts back home were full of legalese. This took the cake.

"Can't you read faster? It's nothing complicated; just standard universal language," she said with a clip of impatience. "Do you need me to translate the translation for you?"

I shot Totty a scowl before turning back to the screen. "I got it." As if I trusted her to point out the parts that would guarantee she could screw me worse than my current situation. I ended up skimming because, honestly, I had to admit it seemed to be written about a hundred IQ points above me. From what I could glean, it specified what Totty could make me do, which seemed to be straightforward. She could make me reclaim assets contracted to Starshine Seizure Specialists, but she couldn't force me to do anything else, like side jobs, marketing, and—thank god—working in the sex trade (even the idea of being a jellybean's sex toy nearly gave me an aneurysm). A sign-on bonus was a reclamation ship with the designation QRX0959UBN.

"This is my ship? As in one hundred percent mine, no strings attached, as long as I work for you until the contract's up?"

"Of course. How else are you going to reclaim assets—by spontaneously developing the ability to fly and soaring across the galaxy wearing a cape?"

I ignored Totty—which I was finding easier to do the longer I was in her company—and continued through the thirty-two-page contract until I reached the signatory page, which caused me to pause. Above a blank, dotted line was another dotted line with my dad's signature: *Caleb Woods*. Next to his signature were two dates, one above the other—at least I assumed the weird string of numbers was a date since the numbers right below it was clearly a date: *July 7, 2009.*

I winced. June 7 was the day my old man had ghosted us. Mom and I had always assumed he walked out on us. It'd hit her hard. She'd once told me that their marriage had been on the rocks, but she'd never thought he would've just got up and left.

I wish she was alive so I could tell her the truth. He hadn't left us, at least not voluntarily. He'd been kidnapped, and I spent a lifetime hating him.

Fifteen years.

For every one of those years, I wondered if he'd show up on our doorstep with arms filled with presents, apologizing for being such a loser, and trying to set things right. He never showed, and he never would.

And I still hated him. Not only did my dad

screw up my life once by disappearing, but he screwed it up again by getting himself killed and signing my life away. I'd never be a truck driver. Sure, not exactly a glamorous job, but it was going to be *my* job.

And now I was just going to be another missing person report—assuming someone even turned me in, but the chance of that was lower than my chance at winning the lottery. My mom was dead and gone. My only friend took the girl who took my virginity. That left my teachers, and let's face it, I'm not the type of student teachers follow up on.

"How do I sign?" I asked glumly.

"With your finger unless you've spontaneously developed telekinesis. What else would you use?"

"You know, you catch more flies with honey than you do with vinegar," I used one of my mother's favorite sayings (I was a mouthy kid) as I signed my name on the screen using the tip of my index finger.

"Why would I want to catch flies? I detest bugs." Totty waddled over.

I took a step to the right to avoid touching her. A part of me wanted to punch the alien to see if she was as squishy as she looked, but another part of me wondered if she had something contagious since she had warty growths on her skin. I hurriedly jotted the date—October 14, 2031—and as soon as I did, a long string of numbers appeared above it. Then I moved away.

"Excellent!" Her high-pitched exclamation caused me to wince. "Welcome to Sunshine Seizure Specialists. You're mine now. Though, legally speaking, you were already mine, but this transfers your father's contract to you. That makes you *more* mine now."

That didn't sound ominous. At all.

The contract on the screen disappeared. "There, I've submitted the contract along with your application to be a reclamation agent. It shouldn't take long—" The screen beeped. "And there it is now. The revised contract's been approved and filed. Congratulations, you're an official reclamation agent, which means that I can get you off my ship and you can start making me some money."

I drew in a slow breath and rubbed my hands together nervously. "All right, so how much do I get paid?"

"It was stipulated in the contract."

"Translate the translation for me," I said, using her earlier words.

"Fine. Payment depends on what you're reclaiming, risk factors, urgency, and more. Every reclamation ticket is unique. In simplest terms, you receive a percentage based on estimated profit."

"Which is?"

"Roughly five percent of the estimated net profit," Totty replied.

I balked. "What? Five percent is nothing!"

"No, zero percent is nothing. This is a substantial five percent. I set the payment rate. You can renegotiate after you successfully complete your first ten tickets. This is all detailed in the contract if you'd taken the time to read it."

"I read it, more or less."

"Obviously, the emphasis on *less*." I swear she

huffed even though she had no mouth. "You're fortunate I'm a generous employer. I'm not legally required to pay my tenured employees more than the minimum required four-point-nine percent rate, anyway."

"Four-point-nine? Wow, you're *so* generous to pay me the extra one tenth of one percent," I said sarcastically.

"I am. And what are you complaining about? Instead of piloting vehicles along straight lines—vehicles that can't even fly, mind you—you get to travel the galaxy."

"That doesn't sound so bad, but since you're saying it like it's a good thing, it's gotta be bad," I said.

"You'll come to appreciate me as your boss. And you know, being a reclamation agent is similar to being a truck driver. Your job is all about transporting goods from point A to point B," she said.

"Truck drivers transport goods that people want. Repo men take stuff that people don't want them to take," I said.

"You're falsely assuming our customers are *people*. SSS works with a highly diverse clientele," she clarified.

"Well, yeah, you mean I could end up with aliens hatching in my belly," I said. As a truck driver, I figured the worst thing I'd catch was chlamydia from a lot lizard (that's a truck stop prostitute for those of you who aren't truck drivers). Not that I'd be hanging out with lizards, I mean.

"There are risks, yes."

Everything about this job made butterflies

churn butter in my stomach. Except that these butterflies were all sting-y, like pissed off wasps.

"Uh, so what happens now?" I asked.

"Now, I need to run scans. I need to ensure you can survive long-term space travel. You belong to an incredibly fragile race," She said.

My hands covered my backside. "Scans? Wait, there aren't going to be anal probes involved, are there?"

"Why would there—oh, never mind. No, just stand there. And quit fidgeting."

After a moment, I asked, "When's the scan start?"

"It's nearly complete," she replied. Another moment passed before she said, "There, it's done. You've passed the health check. And it looks like your nano treatment has been fully absorbed by your cells, which is excellent. Sometimes, there are allergic reactions, but Terran biology seems to be exceptionally well-equipped for accepting foreign objects into their systems."

I twitched. "What nano treatment? I don't remember any type of treatment."

"I gave you your nano treatment when I first brought you onboard, before you regained consciousness. I felt it would be easier that way, and that way you wouldn't reject something necessary for your health. Terran anatomy is not designed for space travel. The radiation would kill you in under three years, and space would damage your brain cells long before that, not that there are many to damage. But I'll have you know, the treatment wasn't cheap. Since you have no cards to your name, I added a year to your contract to cover the expense."

"Gee, thanks. That was mighty generous of you," I said drily. What was another year when I was already committed to sixty-eight years? "What's the nano treatment do, anyway?"

"Just the usual. It defends you against radiation, strengthens your immunity, retains muscle mass, and increases your lifespan. After all, you'll be encountering a wide range of alien systems and biologics, and I want you to stay alive for the term of your contract."

"And hopefully longer," I added.

"Sure, if you decide to extend your contract," she said.

I didn't like Totty very much.

I inspected my forearms and hands, looking for any sign that I'd changed, but my skin looked and felt no different. Seeing that I hadn't developed warts or anything else, I found myself smiling. "I'm like a cybernetic man now? Will these nanites make me stronger, too?"

"Nanites? What are you talking about?"

I frowned, confused. "You said you gave me nanites."

"No, I said I gave you a nano treatment, as in injecting you with something incredibly small. I did *not* inject you with nanites. Do you know how expensive those are?"

"Then what did you inject me with?"

"Tardigrades, of course."

The word was familiar. Then it hit me. "Tardigrades, as in water bears? Like those tiny little organism things? You put *creatures* inside me?"

"They are, though 'creature' is a terribly broad term. And Tardigrades prefer not to be called water bears. Tardigrades are one of the oldest interstellar civilizations and find the term demeaning."

I started scratching my arms, neck, and legs. "You put them inside me?"

"It's a standard procedure for species not physically equipped for space travel."

I scratched more frantically. "Get them out!"

"It's too late. They've already begun establishing a colony inside you. That's how they colonize new systems, by the way. They catch a ride in a host. Rather ingenious approach to colonization if I do say so myself."

"You put parasites inside me?"

"Tardigrades aren't parasitic; they're symbiotic. Do you not understand anything?"

I glared. "Well, considering I was kidnapped by an alien a couple of hours ago, I'd say it's going to take some time to get up to speed on space travel and aliens," I snapped. "I mean it, I'm serious, Totty. Get these things out of me."

"And I'm telling you, I can't. They've already colonized you. There's no removing them."

I shivered. "Are they gonna eat me from the inside out like those Gee eggs did to my dad?" Terror was building in my chest.

I could've sworn Totty rolled her eyes. "I told you, they're symbiotic. They improve their host's capabilities in exchange for a free ride. That's their way to help ensure they get to where they want to go. What good would it do them if you died before they found somewhere they'd like to settle? And when they find such a place, the colony inside you will split, with a few remaining behind to replicate until the next colony, and so on, while the rest emerge from you and colonize the new location."

I held my stomach, imaging an alien bursting forth. "And how do they *emerge* from me, exactly?"

She stared at me. "Do you really need the details?"

"Yes!"

"Fine. You'll expel them via your intestines and through your colon."

The tension slowly melted from my shoulders. Well, that sounded less violent than having my insides ripped apart. Out of all the bombshells I'd been hit with today, this seemed to be the least awful. "How long have you been carrying Tardigrades inside you?"

She shivered. "I'd never let those disgusting little termites in my body."

A ROUND HATCH appeared in the floor, and
Totty waddled toward it. "Now, let's get you to
your ship."

I followed and peered through the small
window in the glass to see a tube and ladder de-
scending into darkness. "Was this thing here this
whole time?"

"I kept a hologram over it while you were running around like a Floid in heat. If you saw the
hatch, I assumed you'd try to do something idiotic
like commandeer a ship that wasn't yours until
you signed the contract," she replied.

I blinked at the hatch. "That's my ship? For
real?"

"Of course. You're obviously not staying on
mine."

"Obviously," I said sarcastically.

Even though the contract had said I got my
own ship, and Totty had said the same thing, I
was still having a hard time believing it.

I squatted to figure out how to open the hatch
when it opened by itself, courtesy of Totty's
freaky telekinetic powers. The tube lit up, re-

vealing a ladder that descended through multiple levels. I stuck my head into the tube and inhaled deeply. The air was breathable and while it was cooler, it wasn't viciously freezing like when I'd opened the other door. I scrambled to spin around to climb down the ladder, but before I descended, I suspiciously eyed Totty. "This really is all mine, like one hundred percent mine?"

"Your brain synapses just don't fire enough, do they? Of course the ship's yours... as long as you don't breach the contract, in which case, I would send another reclamation agent after you and it. I don't get the big deal. It's not like spaceships are hard to come by, especially dumpers like this."

"It's a *spaceship*," I said and then descended the ladder to the first landing. To my left stood a hollow cylindrical space that was so big it made me wonder if it took up a full half of the ship. The right half of the ship looked like it was comprised of three levels based on what I could see from the ladder.

The first floor to my right was a long, cylindrical level lined with cables, pipes, and mechanical thingamajigs. A long gray box the size of two caskets placed end to end had a humming vibration. Another part down a ways reminded me of a giant carburetor, but there was no way a spaceship ran off a combustion engine. Upon closer inspection, I realized that it looked like it processed water since there were water lines going in and out of it. My guess was this level contained all the conduit and cabling that a spaceship would need to run. Strewn everywhere on the floor were boxes of... stuff. Most of it looked like metal junk, but it could've been valuable parts for all I knew.

The next level down wasn't junked up with boxes. A thin Murphy bed was folded out from the wall and a cockpit sat at the far end with a round window that had to be at least four feet in diameter. The main level then. Everything was grimy, scuffed, dented, and battered—far worse than Totty's ship—but that didn't deter my excitement in the least.

I hustled down to the third and final level to find it identical to the top level, with the long casket thingy and everything else. I suppose backups are good ideas in space.

I climbed back up to the middle level and raced to the cockpit. I sat down on the only seat in the small, round cubicle of a cockpit. The bench seat had two waist-only seatbelts, and the dark green cushion was torn and flattened from what looked like decades of hard use. In front of the seat were the ship's computers: two old monitors surrounded by roughly a gazillion buttons and switches.

In awe, I ran my fingers over one of the screens which was constantly scrolling green gibberish. "This is so cool. I can't believe I get my own spaceship. An awesome one at that."

Totty had floated down and was still floating in the air near the ladder. She harrumphed. "It's the opposite of everything awesome. It's a dumper —a relic—and it'll probably break down before you pass through two systems. But that's not my problem. I've fulfilled my end of the contract; now it's your turn. The details of your first ticket are already loaded into the ship's computer, and three courier drones have been placed in the cargo hold so you won't have to return for at least two more tickets. I'll send you your second ticket as soon as you return the asset in a drone. Now, quit acting like a tourist and get to work."

I glanced at the screens before me, "But I don't know how to fly this. I can't even read the gibberish on the screens."

"It flies itself. No bioformic race pilots a ship nowadays. Not even Neptars. The idea is positively preposterous. Pilotage and navigation are what computers are for." She then zoomed upward. I heard the hatch close, and I sprinted toward the ladder. When I looked up, I found the hatch sealed and Totty nowhere in sight.

The sounds of massive metal clamps releasing screeched and caused the ship to shudder, knocking me off my feet. Out of the corner of my eye, I caught movement through the cockpit window. In terror, I jumped to my feet and raced to the cockpit, hopping over a metal crate of switches that someone had bolted to the floor, and to the window to find a light gray, box-shaped spaceship with mismatched round windows drifting away.

Totty.

A second later, a blinding white light shot out from underneath her ship as it raced away, disappearing from my sight.

A squeak escaped me. "Totty!"

She didn't respond, of course, and I stared into the blackness for at least a minute before I accepted the fact that she'd left me high and dry.

I collapsed onto the seat, pushed up my glasses, and stared at screens and buttons before

hard to get an idea when everything's dark outside.

The beeping and flashing continued. "Uh, are those warnings going to go off for the entire trip? Because they're super annoying," I said as I took off my glasses and rubbed my pounding temples.

"Your father had me deactivate them whenever they annoyed him."

I slid my glasses back on. "You can do that?"

"Of course."

When nothing happened, I said, "Uh, can you turn them off?"

The beeping ceased and the red lights disappeared, and I felt relief even though I was basically shoving my head in the sand when it came to the errors.

"Thank you." Was it even appropriate to thank a computer?

"You're most welcome, Frank." She replied in a way that almost sounded sexy, which is not how I'd envisioned a computer to sound like.

"Uh, Fetch, can I ask you a personal question?"

"You can ask me anything. This ship, which includes me, is your asset."

Oh, yeah. That concept would take a while to get used to. "Are you female?"

"I'm a technologic creation. Central supercomputers are neither female nor male nor any other variation of gender. Supercomputers are subcategorized by aspects other than gender, such as craft configuration, operating designation, processing capacity—"

"I get it," I interrupted. "What I mean is why

is your voice so..." Sexy, Sultry, Porn Star-y, Dominatrix-y.

"Feminine?"

"Yeah. That."

"Your father worked with me to establish the voice parameters he preferred. If you dislike the current configuration, we can establish new parameters."

I considered it for a moment. "Nah, I'm good. I kinda like it if you're cool with it."

"Having a voice configuration that pleases you is important as, in all likelihood, you will spend the rest of your life in this ship, alone."

For the past couple of hours, I'd only been able to think ahead one minute at a time. Being kidnapped and coerced into a lifetime contract of forced labor will do that to a guy. So I'd never had the chance to really consider what my life would be like once I was all grown up. When I first entered *Fetch*, I romanticized space travel. I'd pictured zipping out to grab whatever I was hired to grab (from nice aliens, hopefully) and then zipping it off to a pretentious jellybean. Even as I considered that, I knew how stupid that idea was. With how boring it was to drive through Nebraska, how many times worse would it be to fly through the galaxy? At least Nebraska had some changes of scenery to break up the drive. Space was just a bunch of empty... space.

"The rest of my life? That sounds... pathetic."

"Not at all. You have me, and I'm fully versed in emotional and psychological support."

A robot for company? "Gee, thanks. That sounds *so* much better."

"Was that sarcasm?"

"No," I lied.

"It sounded like sarcasm. Your father often applied ironic and caustic remarks like that as well. I consider it a Terran truism," she said.

As she spoke, I realized that she knew my dad a lot better than I did. I hardly remembered him at all. "What was he like, my father?"

"He was ill-tempered. Complaining was his favorite pastime. He never enjoyed his occupation as a reclamation agent, though that could be because he was never any good at it."

"Or maybe because he was blackmailed into doing it like me," I said. "You know, just a few hours ago, I was on my way to class. Life was good." Other than the fact that I'd just found out that my girlfriend was cheating on me with my best friend, I had loans piling up faster than I could make payments, and I generally sucked at life.

"Good? You were eating, sleeping, working, and studying, all within a ten-mile radius. How quaint."

"You make it sound lame. It wasn't lame. It was normal. That's what normal people do."

"We've already traveled a thousand times farther via a hyperlink than you've traveled your first nineteen years on that small planet of yours. Speaking of travel, we're coming up on a mixmaster. You may wish to take a look."

"We've traveled that far already? Wait, what's a mixmaster? Like a giant slushy maker? Oh, I get it. You mean like a giant highway interchange? Wait, what's a hyperlink?" I asked in rapid-fire as I leaned against the window. The glass—though it definitely wasn't glass—surprised me that it wasn't cold.

"A hyperlink is a sub-lightspeed freeway found in inhabited systems and near mixmasters. Without them, ships would experience far more incursions. And yes, you are correct: a mixmaster operates much like a highway interchange on your world. When I translate the universal standard language into your native tongue, I try to find the most fitting words to ease your understanding. Ships must use the mixmasters to travel across many star systems in a short time. Mixmasters hold all accessible warpgates in a particular system."

"That's a lot of big words," I said.

She continued, "And to preemptively answer your next question, warpgates are simply artificial gates that were built to enter warpflows—what your scientists inaccurately coined as worm holes —that were built many eons ago to connect star systems. Nearly every interstellar trip will involve passing through multiple warpgates, which means you'll see more than your fair share of mixmasters and warpgates. In fact, we need to take four warpgates to reach our first destination. We'll spend three days on this first warpflow, two days on the next, eleven days on the one after that, another two days on the fourth warpflow, and four weeks minus two days after the final warpflow."

"Whoa, we'll be flying over a month and a half out there? Wait, are we talking human time or Totty time?"

"I'm using Earth standard time, as it was your father's preference, and I assumed it would be yours as well since you've shown a preference for all his decisions. The other is universal standard time, *not* Totty time. Would you prefer me to give all times in universal standard time instead?"

"No," I answered in a rush. "Let's stick with Earth time for now."

"As you wish, Frank."

At first, I didn't notice anything, but as we flew, what I thought were twinkling stars morphed into ships queued in at least a dozen curved lines. The lines reminded me of rush hour traffic only with spaceships instead of cars, but where rush hour traffic went on for a few miles, these lines seemed to go on forever and, instead of bumper to bumper, there must've been a hundred miles between each ship. In space, a hundred miles *looked* bumper to bumper. I felt *Fetch* lurch as it slid in behind another ship. There were at least twenty ships in front of us, but they were moving so fast, and disappeared just as fast through what I assumed was the warpgate, faster than I could count them. The warpgate was a thick gray ring outlined with hollow gray triangles that seemed to be just floating in space. The center looked like space, too, only different. There were more stars and what looked like a nebula.

As each ship passed through the gate, it vanished in a flash of light.

When we were next in line, a flurry of text scrawled down one screen, followed by a beep. I tensed. "What just happened?"

"They deducted the toll fees from your account. Well, it was your father's account, but, like me, it was transferred to you upon his death. I should advise you, your father's account was dangerously close to being overextended. You have enough to pay the tolls on this trip, but you desperately need more cards to buy food and supplies."

"Cards?"

"'Money' in your common language, I believe."

That my dad didn't leave me much money didn't surprise me. Mom had often complained about how he'd spent every extra cent before he walked out, er, was taken. What surprised me was the extent of capitalism in the universe. "We have to pay a toll to use a warpgate?"

"We have to pay a toll to use *every* warpgate."

I grunted. "Figures. Let me guess, we have to pay taxes, too."

"Only local taxes, depending on the local economy. GOD does not tax."

"Amen," I said.

"You'd better secure yourself. Passing through warpgates can be a little jarring," Fetch said.

I scrambled for the seatbelt, but we crossed the warpgate before I could fasten it. I wasn't thrown back. It was worse. The ship's gravity didn't just disappear, I was pulled toward the front of the ship. I smashed into the window, only to slide down to the floor as things leveled out. My stomach felt like it was in my throat, and I thought I was going to throw up before it settled back to where it was supposed to be. Somehow, I managed not to puke.

I groaned as I pulled myself up and onto the seat. I righted my glasses and looked out the window to see lights flashing by. It was too much, and I threw up all over myself.

"As I cautioned, warpgates can be jarring to bioforms," Fetch said. "The good news is you have three days until we cross through this warpflow's far warpgate. We're officially traversing the intergalactic Space-Link network."

"Whatever," I muttered as I wiped my mouth. "Tell me this ship has a shower."

"I can tell you that if you'd like, but I would be lying," she said.

I blanched. "What? There's no shower?"

"I said, I can tell you—"

"No, I mean, are you for real? There's no shower?" I sucked in a breath. "Not even a bathtub? Tell me it isn't so."

"There are no bathing facilities on this ship. However, there is a sink and a lavatory for your use. They are located next to your sleeping platform."

I stared blankly ahead. I still dreaded the idea of never being able to go home, even if my home sucked. But all that angst didn't come close to the level of stress I felt at the idea of never having a bath ever again. Quite possibly my favorite thing in the entire world was taking a long, hot bubble bath. I *love* my baths. I might've even used a scented candle or two. My mom used to take a bubble bath every night, and her habit rubbed off on me. A psychologist would probably tell me I loved baths as a way of staying connected with my mother since she died when I was so young, but honestly, I think it's because I just love baths.

"I sense you are stressed," Fetch said.

"No shit? Wow, you must have some really good sensors to tell that," I snapped back.

"There's that sarcasm again."

I blew out a breath rather than snap back, and I recoiled when I smelled my own breath and stench. "Tell me, are there at least some extra clothes around here somewhere, maybe even a toothbrush?"

"All of your father's belongings are here. However, he did not have a toothbrush—he used algae tablets for cleaning his mouth."

My lower lip curled in disgust. "Algae tablets?"

"They are cheap and do an excellent job at protecting enamel. They are the standard teeth-cleaning device for travelers."

"If you say so." No longer nauseous, I pulled off my stained shirt and used it to mop up my vomit. As I got down on my knees and wiped, I muttered, "It'd be nice if the Tardigrades kept me from puking."

"You received Tardigrades?"

"Yeah, why?"

"They are excellent protection against radiation, but in response, they tend to cause more purging of impurities. Your father was not a fan of them," Fetch replied.

I rolled from my knees to my butt. "What do you mean by purging, like puking?"

"I mean you will evacuate your bowels more frequently."

I groaned. "My life is literally going down the crapper."

"I see you inherited your father's humor. I

obviously don't need to activate my humor response sound," she said.

I finished wiping up my mess and climbed to my feet. "Please tell me, there's some sort of laundry facilities on this ship."

"You'll find a personal-sized cleaning station next to the food station. It cleans clothes, dining material, and even tools. It's on this level with all living operational systems. You've walked or run past it five times already."

I started walking down the passageway.

"Six times."

I paused and turned. On the wall to my right was what I assumed to be the cleaning station since a bin magically opened, courtesy of Fetch. I flung my shirt into the bin. It closed and the screen above it lit up, and the words, "Wash in Progress" displayed.

"Clothes are in the cabinets under and above the bed," she said.

The cabinets were right across from me. I rummaged until I found a stained, wrinkled shirt and slid it on. As I did, I asked, "Hey, where are we going, anyway?"

"Totty didn't tell you?"

"Nope."

"I'm not surprised. Totty tends to not go beyond the minimum level of effort for her agents," she said. "Your first ticket is to reclaim a computer."

I grunted. "Repoing a computer doesn't sound very hard."

"It isn't. It's an excellent first ticket for a new agent. An errant youth stole the computer from his father when he ran away from home. The youth clearly didn't realize that his ship has a ge-otag installed. We have his exact coordinates."

I shrugged. "You know, maybe this job won't be so bad after all."

"That's an optimistic way of looking at it. Since you're a new reclamation agent, statisti-cally, no one really expects you to live beyond the first three tickets, anyway. That's why Totty pro-vided only three return drones."

5 / GO FAST, TURN LEFT

EIGHT DAYS and four warpgates later

"Fetch, is there a thingamajig around here that fits this whatchamacallit?" I asked while I lay on my back and kept trying—futilely—to hand-tighten an overly thick bolt-like fastener under the leaky sink.

"Your grasp of the English language is incredible, and by incredible, I mean it is both horrendous and ludicrous," Fetch said.

My hand slipped, which caused the fastener to fall off the pipe. Water splashed my face. I muttered curses as I took off my glasses and wiped them on my shirt. After my rant, I slid the fastener back into place, slowing the stream to a *drip-drip-drip* again.

"If it boosts your ego, I should add that your grasp of the English language is an improvement over your mechanical skills," she said.

"Not helping." I scowled at the ceiling, where I assumed one of her gazillion cameras and speakers was placed, not that I'd seen any yet. She'd said there were just as many cameras placed outside, which had come in handy to get a feel for what my ship looked like inside and out.

I think she would've sighed if she had lungs... or even rolled her eyes if she had eyes (unless the cameras counted as eyes). "Yes, there is a thinga-majig called a carabiner wrench in the toolbox on level 3, and it's designed to work on all carabiner bolts. It should be right next to the last three tools you pulled out of the toolbox."

Spaceships didn't technically have upper and lower decks since there's no up or down in space. *Fetch* had been built in standard reclamation ship configuration. It consisted of two major sections: the front half contained three levels stacked on top of each other while the back half was an open cargo space. I didn't know what I'd ever pick up that would fill that space, but I had it if I needed it.

So far, I kept gravity turned on throughout the ship, albeit slightly under Earth's normal gravity. I disliked zero-G for two reasons. First, every-thing takes ten times as long to do, especially when you're not athletically gifted (like me). And second—even more importantly—zero-G makes me puke.

Artificial gravity is a huge step up from zero-G, but it's still nowhere close to the real thing. Yesterday, Fetch had spent a half-hour telling me about how artificial gravity worked, or at least until I fell asleep. From what I remembered, arti-ficial gravity had something to do with the rein-forced walkways being made of heavier-than-normal matter while the "ceilings" contained a thin film of antimatter. The two types of matter worked in a way that the floor pulled me down. I could walk just like I could on Earth, but there were some quirks. Artificial gravity's stronger the closer you are to the floor, so sweat on my face often stayed there instead of running down. I was always congested, like I had allergies, since my head sinuses wouldn't drain right. On the plus side, since the gravity lessened as the distance grew from the floor, I could carry things twice as heavy as I could back on Earth—if I could lift it from the floor, that was.

I pushed myself out from under the sink and set the half-filled bowl back under the pipe. I rolled to my feet, stretching my arms and back once I did so. My biceps burned from working down low where gravity was greatest. I took a swig of water directly from the faucet. When I turned off the faucet, I could hear the constant *drip-drip-drip* that had been haunting my dreams as much as during my waking hours. When there was no one else onboard except for a know-it-all computer, other sounds really came to the forefront.

I think my ears had become more sensitive over the past week. At first, all I could hear was a constant thrum of the engines, but within a day or so, I could discern that the thrum was a symphony of system sounds. I was no expert on what systems made what sounds, but I'd become awfully familiar with the systems that weren't running smoothly.

The plumbing leaked, and I'm not talking about just the sink. The toilet leaked, too, which was extra disgusting since it didn't even use water, and worse, because Fetch had been right: Tardigrades make you poop often and *vigorously*.

At least the sink and toilet still functioned for the most part (knock on wood or whatever composite material that everything in the ship seemed to be made of).

The other system bugs scared me more. The propulsion system on engine number two had a hitch in it that clanked every hour—or as Fetch pointed out, every ten-thousandth rotation. Every time it did, I wondered if that would be the time the engine would quit. There were plenty of other bugs, too, which Fetch was prioritizing on the already insanely long error log. Every bug on that list required A) parts we didn't have, B) a specialist to fix it, or C) all the above. So far, all the bugs except for the plumbing problems were "all the above," and I was beginning to have doubts about learning these skills fast enough. I'd fixed leaky pipes in my apartment before—how hard could it be to do the same thing on an alien spaceship?

Evidently, pretty freaking hard.

I trudged down to the lower deck, i.e. level 3, to where all the tools and replacement parts were stored. I know it's weird that the "top" floor is called level 2 while the "bottom" floor is level 3 (evidently, the center, main floor is always level 1), but I guess that's standard spaceship design. And since I didn't take Spaceship Design Fundamentals 101 at community college, I just went with it. Weird level numbers was the easiest thing to learn so far.

Calling the toolbox a "box" was a bit of a misnomer though. The ship's toolbox was actually a built-in row of narrow compartments that ran the entire length of the wall.

I'd become familiar with the toolbox over the past week. After spending the first few hours touring the ship, I learned that Totty had been right. This ship was a piece of crap that had been held together with the intergalactic equivalent of duct tape, spit, and maybe even a miracle or two.

I walked along the wall until I reached the compartment with the other plumbing tools. I rifled through the compartment, looking for something that would fit the odd bolt around the sink pipe. After a minute, I grumbled. "Uh, what's this thingamajig supposed to look like?

"It's supposed to look like a carabiner wrench," Fetch replied through a speaker somewhere above my head.

"And that would look like...?"

"A short-handled gray tool with a fixed crescent opening and a movable crescent side."

I rummaged through the compartment again. "I don't see anything that looks like that."

"Check the compartment to your right," she offered.

I did, but that was filled with tapes and glues. "Nothing."

"Check the other adjoining compartment," she said.

I did, but that was filled with rags, broken tools, and basically, well, just junk. "Still nothing."

"Check your other right."

My brow came together. "You mean my left?"

"Yes."

"Then why didn't you say 'left?'"

"I enjoy watching you look confused. You're a cute little pet."

I bristled. "I am not your *pet*."

"You're completely reliant upon me. you do what I tell you to do, you're mostly housebroken, and I can make you perform silly tricks. That sounds exactly like a pet to me."

"Well, I disagree. Plus, that's just mean." I loudly rifled through the compartment to the left of the one I'd first opened. I yanked out a tool that resembled a large crescent wrench with a floppy second crescent wrench part hanging loosely from it. As I held it up, the loose part swung back and forth. "Hey, is this it?"

"It is."

"Is this all I need?" I asked as I continued to swing it through the air like a nunchuck.

"Yes, but you must put it on the bolt for it to work. Playing with it won't fix anything, but you could manage to give yourself a black eye."

"I'm not *that* clumsy," I said.

"I'd beg to differ. Do you want me to play back the video I recorded of you attempting to re-knit the holding nets in the cargo bay and you wound up bouncing off the walls for ten minutes?"

"In my defense, there's barely any gravity back there," I countered. "On the plus side, I learned the first rule of space travel: I'm not Superman. Things have gone a lot better since then." I puked a lot less, for one thing.

"Better? How about the incident on level 2 when you were strapping the cables together and accidentally strapped your arm to the cables?"

It'd taken me three hours to escape from that stupid strap. After that, I started carrying a rusty knife I'd found in the toolbox.

"You have a very narrow view of life expansionism."

I began pacing the walkway. "That's because I've been in space for all of eight days. So far, I've been blackmailed into taking over my dad's job—this is a dad I don't even remember, mind you, and all I know about him are some pretty nasty things my mom said before she died. After that, all I've been doing is fixing a spaceship. I'm not a spaceship mechanic."

"You've certainly proven that you are not."

"And the only person I have to keep me company isn't even a person. It's a sarcastic, know-it-all supercomputer."

"The term 'sarcastic' seems to be a criticism, while 'know-it-all' is a compliment. I'll accept the latter and reject the former. Thank you."

"You're welcome." I stopped at a section in the wall that had a screen surrounded by buttons. Below it was a spout and a small shelf. I tapped a sequence of buttons to select *Caleb's Favorite #5*. From behind the screen came a whir. I scrambled to grab a bowl from the cabinet and set it on the shelf. As soon as I did, brown sludge that resembled chunky chocolate ice cream squirted into the bowl. I wished it was ice cream. Instead, it was an entire buffet of flavors—from chalk to cardboard to something akin to liver. Surprisingly, it had never made me gag.

What I really missed was steak. You see, space has this smell to it. Sometimes, it reminds me of burnt metal, but sometimes it reminds me of seared steak. And every time I get that whiff, my mouth would water. I'd kill to find a good steakhouse. Instead, I had to eat cardboard sludge with textured chalk flakes.

Even with all the flavors, the food was bland, which Fetch said could've been because my body was still adjusting to the nuances of space. For example, even though there was artificial gravity in the floor, my body still knew we were in zero-G, so my sinuses never quite cleared right.

Then again, the food might've tasted off because the slop that came out of the food station—I called it the foodie—produced something I was being extremely generous in calling it food.

Which is why I kept working off my dad's recipe list since I hadn't found a single thing worth adding to my list yet. At least his favorite items didn't cause bathroom issues like Fetch's first "dietary recommendation" she'd made for me. I spent four extra hours on the toilet, no thanks to her helpful advice.

I made my way to the cockpit, which had the only chair in the entire ship. I propped my feet on the instrument panel. As I did so, an idea struck. "Hey, Fetch, add 'hammock' to the problem log."

"I don't understand. This ship has no hammock."

"Exactly. And that's a problem."

"I'm not sure how to prioritize nonexistent problems," Fetch mused.

"I guess, put it somewhere below the printer part and above the burned-out light in the cargo hold."

"There are one hundred and twenty-nine items between the printer and lightbulb," she said.

"Well," I drawled. "Put it somewhere in the top quarter."

"Consider it done, o wise one," she said.

I cocked my head. "Are you making fun of me?"

"I'm a supercomputer. Why would I make fun of you? I have more important things to do, like flying this ship and keeping you alive."

"You'd better keep me alive. I'm not exactly up to speed on surviving the dark depths of space yet."

"Your body will never allow you to survive the space outside," she said.

"I know that. I meant—never mind."

"Keeping you alive is far easier than running this ship. When it comes to space travel, bioforms more often die from starvation rather than from exposure as a result of life support equipment failure. As long as you don't do something idiotic like cut a hole in the hull, I can assure you that our food supply will feed you for seven hundred and sixty-one of your Earth days."

"Just 'cause we have enough food, don't slack off on the life support. Breathing and heat are kind of important things to me," I said.

"Your wellbeing is my priority. After all, should you perish, I'd have to transport your corpse back to Triple-S docks and then be sold to who knows what. I've come to enjoy flying with Terrans. You are more trainable than most species."

"Uh, thanks?" I said, as I slurped another spoonful of brown sludge.

After I swallowed, something struck me.

"Hey, Fetch, I just realized something. I have no idea what you look like."

"Yes, you do. You're looking at me now."

I looked at the instrument panel. "What, you mean you're the panel?"

"No." It was amazing how a computer could fill a single word with exasperation. "I am fully integrated with the ship so that everything you see and interface with—every cable, screen, sensor—you're also interfacing with me. I could not be removed from this ship just as the ship could never fly without me. I am the ship, and the ship is me."

"Even the plumbing?"

"I'm integrated with the plumbing systems, of course."

I chuckled. "So it's your job to literally deal with my shit every day?"

"Figuratively and literally, Frank. Tell me, Frank. Would that count as humor on your home world?"

I shrugged. "My roommate would laugh at something like that." I didn't point out that Jacob had the emotional maturity of a five-year-old.

There was a beep, and I jumped, nearly dropping the bowl. "What was that?"

"We have received a message from Totty. She demands a status update," Fetch announced.

"Tell her to suck it. I'm working on it," I said.

"Okay. Reply sent."

My feet hit the floor. "Wa..., wa..., wait., What? You didn't send that, did you?"

"Of course. Your wish is my command."

I rubbed my temple with my free hand. "At least it'll take, what, days, weeks, before it reaches her, right? By the time she replies, I can think of something nice to say."

"She received your message, and she's already replied, citing that disrespecting one's superior is grounds for termination, and she's demanding a complete and proper status update," she said.

I shivered even though it was warm on the ship. "How'd she reply so fast? We're lightyears away. Wait, we *are* lightyears away from Totty, aren't we?"

"Yes. Her communication originated in the Yulang sector. However, all standard space communications leverage QuSR technology standards—that stands for Quantum Splitter Relay—which allows for near-instantaneous data packet transfers across multiple systems. It doesn't allow for voice or video communications that your kind so adores, but very few races prefer voice or video to data as it is incredibly inefficient."

"Thanks for the tech lesson. All you had to say was yeah, I can't use the old 'the check's in the mail' excuse with Totty," I said drily. A headache loomed. I pressed my fist against my forehead and clenched my eyes shut. "Well, heck. Can you send her a nice apology for me, so she doesn't send someone to kill me or something?"

"I can, but I have a better idea," Fetch offered.

I looked up. "Okay, shoot."

"I have no weapons."

"I was speaking figuratively," I said.

"I know. I've picked up many Earth witticisms from your father as well as from radio waves and satellite data emitted from your world. But I enjoy that you've brought me a wealth of new ones."

"Your idea?" I asked, anxious.

"Don't send her a response. I assure you, she won't like anything you send, anyway."

"I can't do that. She already knows I got her message. And she said she'd terminate me."

"You are one of her assets. She will not terminate you. It is hard to get paperwork to bring in new repo agents, and Totty knows it. Therefore, she won't terminate any of her agents," she said.

"That's reassuring, I guess."

"Instead, she'll assign the worst tickets to the subpar agents so that they're killed on the job, so she can then get approval to replace the agent. There's too much paperwork involved in terminating her own agents. Plus, it's bad for recruitment."

"And she expects me to die on the job," I muttered.

"Statistically, that's a near-certainty," she said. "However, your odds of survival improve as you complete more tickets," she said in what sounded like the first empathetic statement I'd heard from a computer that was supposedly versed in being the emotional caretaker for her crew.

She continued, "As for my idea, your father often had me disable our communications network. Totty would not find it odd if you, too, encountered communication problems on the same ship."

I frowned. "But if they're off, we can't reach anyone if we need to, and no one can reach us."

"From whom are you expecting a call?" she asked.

"Ouch. Point to Fetch," I said, rubbing my heart.

I considered her idea for a moment and then shrugged. "All right, fine, let's do it. Turn off the comms."

"I already did. I knew my plan was the best option, so I disabled them as soon as Totty's second message arrived."

There was another beep, and I sighed. "I thought you said you turned off the comms."

"I did. That wasn't an incoming data packet. It's a proximity alert," she replied.

I jerked forward. "What?"

"My sensors have indicated a dark matter clump in our flight path. They aren't uncommon as they are created in warpflows as a result of energy surges distributed unevenly from heavy traffic. We are traveling too fast and are already too close to avert it. Our scanners are what you'd call bottom-dollar, as that is what your father could afford. The problem with low-powered scanners is that they cannot catch all issues in adequate time."

"That sounds like a seriously big problem," I said.

"It can be. This is one of those situations where your father would've had me ask him if he wanted the good news or the bad news first."

"Uh, okay. Always give me the bad news first. I like to have something to look forward to."

"The bad news is that black matter clumps don't play well with graphene and tend to cause system issues."

"Let me guess, this ship has graphene?" I asked.

"Our entire hull is wrapped in a graphene web. It serves as the ship's battery. The inner walls and cables are also all wrapped in graphene webbing, as it's the most efficient source for wiring and power."

"That sounds bad," I said.

"It is. We will have system issues, but that brings us to the good news. Dark matter clumps don't destroy ships."

I shrugged. "That actually sounds like good news to me."

"It is for a technoform. Dark matter clumps don't bode as well for bioforms," Fetch said.

"Aw, c'mon. Now, why'd you go and say that?"

Instead of commenting, she said, "Hold on. We're entering the black matter clump now."

The space outside became a tar pit. A second later, the ship went dark as all systems shut down.

floor. My arms felt weightless, and my hands were drifting loosely. So that's what Fetch had meant about magnetic boots. Awesome invention.

I took a couple of steps, and my boots connected with the floor each time with a *click*. I glanced at the sole of one of my boots to see a gray magnetized metal built into the heel. That made life easier, but even with mag-boots, walking was awkward. If I didn't take high steps, the magnets in my heels would snap to the floor too soon, and I'd end up taking jerky baby steps. You don't realize how much gravity plays a role in every movement until it's gone. I wobbled like a drunk man with every step I took, trying to find my balance. No wonder Fetch had said artificial gravity was a required feature on all ships that carried crews. I would've gone insane by now if this ship never had it.

When I reached my bunk, I realized I couldn't simply lie down, not without floating away. I stood next to the bunk for a few seconds when it finally hit me. In the wall alongside the bed were three long straps that pulled out from and auto retracted into the wall. On the end of each strap was a large hook. I'd pulled at the straps a few times after going to bed, trying to figure out what use they could possibly serve. Now that I looked at them, their purpose was obvious.

I held myself to the bed with one hand while pulling my feet off the floor, which turned out to be harder than I ever would've guessed. After some clumsy shifting, I managed to hold myself more or less prone on my bed. I scrambled to pull out a strap with one hand while holding the bed rail with my other. I then hooked the strap to the rail, and the strap tightened enough to press me into the bed. The next two straps were easier, and I ended up cocooned into the bed. The straps were snug but also had some give, so I could move, but my helmet made lying on my side awkward. I finally settled on my back.

With my headlamp shining on the ceiling, I turned off the light and lay in the darkness.

My breathing through the suit's airways was so loud in my ears that it reminded me of the whoosh of a truck's air brakes, which then reminded me of how far I'd left my old life. I'd been less than a month away from getting teamed up with a truck driver on a real job. Safe to say that was never going to happen now.

I suppose flying a spaceship is a little like driving a truck. I was alone, only instead of driving on a highway, I was riding an intergalactic wormhole. But I definitely wasn't my own boss. As if kidnapping me didn't make that fact obvious, Totty had made it abundantly clear that I was her indentured servant. At least I got a spaceship out of the deal. Though I'd like it a lot better if it actually worked.

As I lay there, I wondered how many times my dad had been in this exact position, strapped in this cocoon in the dark, hoping for Fetch to come back online. She'd obviously come back online every time for Dad, so that had to be a good sign, right?

I kept my fingers crossed.

The suit was a lot more comfortable when I was standing—it had too many lumps and pokey things pressing into my back when I was horizontal, not to mention, every breath made me sound like Darth Vader which was both distracting and a reminder that it was the only thing keeping me alive. After a while, the bed straps felt more bondage and less cocoon. But I was exhausted enough that I fell asleep eventually.

When I woke, the ship was still dark, and that got my nerves amped up. Hello, cortisol. I wondered if the Tardigrades saw that as an impurity to filter—I guess I'd find out if I had to poop in the next ten minutes. Other than cursing them every time I used the bathroom, I didn't think about the little bugs much anymore.

"Fetch?" I called out, but I didn't expect to receive a response.

I checked my HUD. Evidently spacesuits have a lot better battery packs than cell phones since my suit was showing at ninety-four percent power. I assumed that single reading applied to air, heat, pressure, and everything else the suit had to do to keep me alive. At least I sure hoped it did, because I had no idea how to run the damn thing.

———

Guess what?

I learned how to run the damn thing. Six full days passed with no hint of Fetch or ship power, which gave me a lot of time to become 1) paranoid, and 2) intimately familiar with my hab-suit. I now knew how to shake my head back just right to *sort of* slide my glasses up my nose. I also figured out how the privy system worked and how to eject waste using the wall system next to the suit's locker.

I even figured out how to eat and drink. I discovered a long, flexible straw that retracted into the helmet. When I pulled it out, a straw popped out inside my helmet as well. Mealtime took a full thirty minutes each time since sucking goop through a straw takes effort, and I had to take breaks or else I'd get lightheaded. As long as I drank my food, I could live indefinitely in the suit. But man, I missed cheeseburgers and pizza... and pretty much every food imaginable back on Earth. Shoot, by day four, I was missing the glop that the ship's food machine made. Man was not made for a liquid diet.

When I wasn't sucking down my meals or ejecting my waste, I stayed busy with random busyness. I could tell you what was tucked in every drawer and in every nook and cranny across the ship. I'd been searching for an operator's manual (didn't find one) but found plenty of other interesting things. I even found an honest-to-god *blaster* hidden in a small wall cabinet. I knew it was a blaster because it was sitting on a charging pad, and regular guns didn't need that. The belt and holster fit, though I had to add a notch to the belt to make it tight enough. My dad had clearly cultivated a beer gut. I wore the blaster around the ship for a few hours, practicing drawing, before growing bored with even that, and putting it back on its charger. With my luck, I'd accidentally shoot a hole through the hull, making my problems even worse.

Why my dad had a blaster, I had no idea. Maybe he had one because he thought people in

"I'm not crazy," I replied.

"That's debatable. If you're not crazy, your risk-taking tolerance certainly is. I find those odds problematically high. In my experience, one percent can become ninety-nine percent within a moment, and one point three percent can become one hundred percent in an instant."

"But we're ninety-nine percent likely to make the warpgate. I'll take that as good news any day of the week and thrice on Sunday," I said.

"Thrice? Is that word even used in your language anymore?"

I shrugged. "I like to bring back the good stuff."

"Should nothing catastrophic happen and we reach the warpgate, we'll also reach the designated system faster, just not thrice as fast," she added.

I cocked my head. "Then why didn't we plan on taking those warpgates the first time?"

"Because with every warpgate, we pay a toll, and your father's directive was to always take the cheaper route."

"We have enough money, er, cards, I mean, to cover the tolls, right?" I asked.

"We do."

"Okay, so there's no problem." I crossed my arms over my chest but found it awkward since I was still wearing my hab-suit. I went to remove my helmet, but an alarm beeped, and I jumped.

I glanced around. "What was that?"

"That was me getting your attention. I highly recommend that you do not unseal your suit. While the air is breathable, albeit thin, the temperature on this ship is currently negative fifty-six degrees Celsius, that would be negative sixty-eight point eight degrees Fahrenheit in your neck of the woods. You might find that rather brisk in the bare moments before you freeze to death."

"Oh." I lowered my hands. "Good to know."

"I recommend you take a seat and buckle in. You don't want to end up smashed against the window again as we traverse the next warpgate, do you?" she asked.

"You saw that?"

"I see everything aboard my ship. I also hear everything. You are quite entertaining to listen to, but I must say, I'm not sure about your singing ability."

I made my way to the cockpit and noticed that only half of the screens and buttons were lit up. I pointed to them. "Hey, Fetch, is that a problem?"

"We're running off minimal systems. We have multiple problems to resolve from the damage the black matter clump caused, so I can't infer what specific problem you may be addressing. But we have enough functionality to traverse the warpflow and warpgates... for now."

I gestured. "See? Now why did you have to go and say that 'for now' bit? C'mon, Fetch, what're you trying to do, foreshadow like we're characters in some horror flick?"

"You've watched too many movies. The worst that can happen—"

"Is that I can die, or we can be trapped in a warpflow forever? Yeah, I kinda got that already. I just want you to be a bit more optimistic. You're supposed to be programmed to provide emotional support, and I'm telling you, I'm deeply emotionally vulnerable right now."

"I give you the support you require with full honesty. Would you prefer that I mislead you?"

I weighed the pros and cons of that, but before I could answer, she said, "Okay, Frank. Everything's fine. You have nothing to worry about."

"Hey, now you're just placating me. And yeah, I know big words like that," I said, grumbling.

"I don't believe two-syllable words are considered 'big' words in any Terran language."

I decided computers across the universe had a knack for making people feel dumb. "Okay, listen, I'm cool with your ruthless honesty, but maybe you can give it to me in a sandwich."

"I do not understand."

"You know, sandwich the bad news in between some good news."

"I will try my best, oh captain of mine."

I cocked my head. "Was that snark? Because that definitely sounded like snark to me."

She didn't answer. Instead, she said, "Warpgate entry in ten seconds. Sit back and prepare for the transference shift."

Data flowed across the one screen that was operational. Since Fetch could fly herself, I felt like I wasn't necessary. Kind of like that role Sigourney Weaver plays on *Galaxy Quest*, where all she did was repeat things that the ship said. Maybe I'd do that with Fetch if she started annoying me. The idea made me smile.

Even with her talking down to me, it felt good to have Fetch back. I hadn't realized how stressed

I was until she came back online. My muscles ached from being tense all the time, and I battled with a never-ending migraine. I was exhausted and antsy, like a sloth with ADHD.

I remained quiet and watched as we closed the distance on the small warpgate glowing straight ahead. Warpgates looked like tiny black holes surrounded by an aurora borealis. They were cool and spooky at the same time. The closer we got, the bigger the hole grew...the rate of the hole's growth reminding me just how fast we were flying. I still didn't get the concept of warpflows, even after Fetch had explained the concept to me at least a dozen times. Somehow, we weren't flying at lightspeed because most bio-forms (her term, not mine) can't survive the radiation that bombards a ship and crew at faster-than-light speeds, even with Tardigrades constantly feeding off the stellar radiation passing through my body.

Despite our speed, we were traveling from Point A to Point B *faster* than lightspeed. Something about the warpflows being hyperlinks through multiple, parallel universes which drastically cut down the distance we needed to cover.

Yeah, it's confusing.

Even with warpflows and lightyears of distance saved, there was still a ton of time spent traveling from one system to another. For one thing, there were no-warp zones around any habited planet or station. Since there were dozens of interstellar species who'd been busy colonizing the galaxy, there were roughly a gazillion no-warp zones.

I clenched the armrests as we passed through

the warpgate and entered a mixmaster. My ears always popped entering and leaving a warpflow, which I assumed meant there were pressure differences in addition to the general rocking and shaking of the ship. And, for the first five minutes after leaving a warpflow, I felt a little lightheaded and wobbly. After the first warpgate we'd taken, I'd left my seat only to face plant the floor. I stayed in my seat after that.

Mixmasters were fascinating, alien architectures. Every mixmaster had a unique structure based on how many warpgates it had. This one had a lot, and I could see several dozen ships, probably more, lining up and moving through the various warpgates. Doorways on earth were generally vertical, while things like manhole covers were horizontal. But since space isn't hindered by a little thing called gravity, warpgates can be planted in every direction. Mixmasters looked like the Mad Hatter designed them.

We proceeded to the lower left (that's the closest direction I could perceive from my cockpit window, anyway) while most ships were traveling toward the upper right warpgates.

"It's like we're in a stock car race," I said.

"What do you mean?" she asked.

"Go fast, turn left," I replied as if that would explain everything. It didn't.

"Did you strike your head on something?" she asked.

"No, and your cameras would've seen it if I had. What I meant was that in stock car races, the cars just travel in a big loop where they drive fast and then turn to the left for the entire race."

"That sounds boring."

"They go *really* fast," I clarified.

"As fast as we're going now?" she asked.

"Well, no."

"Then, I reiterate, that sounds boring."

Before I could explain any further about cars passing each other and crashing into each other or the wall, a beeping burst from the speakers, and I pitched forward. "What was that?"

"We've been hailed by GOD," Fetch replied.

I rolled my eyes. "God—that's a good one. Seriously, what's going on?"

"As I told you, we've been hailed by GOD—according to their credentials, a GOD Auditor, to be precise."

I stared blankly at the screen. "God's real, and he's hailing us?"

"Of course, though I don't understand why the concept intrigues you so. The Galactic Oversight Directorate is the galaxy's governing force. GOD is the elder race of technoforms that oversees the consortium of space-faring species, specifically space travel and colonization. They toured the galaxy long before any other race traveled the stars, and established regulations for a safe and shared galaxy."

I considered Fetch's words. "So... back on Earth, a lot of people pray to this guy called God." My mom had taken me through a lot of religions on her journey to find personal enlightenment, including a couple variations of Christian denominations. In the end, she'd finally settled on some new age version of Buddhism after chemotherapy failed and she'd given up on colon cancer treatments.

"The name likely came from a traveler,

maybe even a GOD drone, who visited your planet at some point in your race's history."

"Huh, how about that. God's a computer."

"If there was an entity worth praying to, of course it would be a computer," said the computer. "Now, if you'll excuse me, I need to focus on docking with the Auditor."

"Wha, wait a sec. We're docking to another ship?" I asked.

"Yes. When GOD hails you with a request to dock, it is always best to comply," she replied.

"What are they going to do to us?"

"They've reported that they conducted an inspection of this ship and are docking for a reason that cannot be communicated via normal channels."

"That sounds bad. Is it bad?"

"In all likelihood, yes," she said.

I winced. "Remember the sandwich."

"Frank, you are about to have the honor of meeting a drone of GOD. Unfortunately, they will likely either ground us or fine us. But you get to meet a drone of GOD. How's that for a sandwich?"

"We're going to have to work on your delivery."

The sound of something solid bumping into my ship led me to suck in a quick breath.

"They've attached, and I'm showing a seal. They are entering through the hatch on level 1. I've already relayed information about your race and your pertinent individual details. It is customary for the captain of the ship to greet them."

"And that's me, I guess." I unlatched my seatbelt and jumped to my feet nervously. The only other alien I'd met was Totty, and she threatened to kill me after letting me nearly walk out of an airlock. She's pretty scary for a purple jellybean. What in the world would an alien called GOD be like?

Turns out, kind of dorky.

The GOD drone floated in through the open airlock, and I was surprised to find it was less than two feet tall. It looked more humanlike than Totty, but that wasn't saying much. It had a head, torso, and two arms like humans did, but that was where any similarities ended. It had two huge, bulging, glass-like eyes and then another two smaller eyes where its ears should've been. Lines of code flickered through each of the orbs. This thing was clearly robotic in nature, made of some kind of translucent bronze metal I didn't recognize. Within the metal shell of its torso, lights flickered and ran through its body like blood through a blood vessel. Each of its hands had dozens of tendril-like fingers. With the torso ending with a pointed bottom, I wouldn't have been surprised if it could spin like a top. Without legs, it looked to be only half-completed, but I guess you don't need legs when you can float.

"Um, hi." I gave a small wave. "Welcome to my ship?" I had no idea if the GOD drone even spoke English.

"Salutations, Terran bioform of the Sol system," it replied in a voice that sounded as artificial as the drone looked, yet authoritatively masculine. "I am a formally recognized representative of the Galactic Oversight Directorate, Extraterrestrial Public Relations Division. For your convenience, you may refer to me using my abridged unique identifier, J'zchk'kv."

I wrinkled my brow. That was its *abridged* name? "Jiz-ch-what?"

"J'zchk'kv."

I tried again. "Jiz-chuck-kiv?"

"No, J'zchk'kv."

I frowned. "That's what I said."

"No. You put too much emphasis on the second syllable when the first and third syllables are dominant."

I tried its name on my lips a couple of times before I finally said, "How about I just call you Jack?"

"I find the inaccurate moniker acceptable, given your race's linguistic limitations."

"Um, thanks, I guess?"

It floated toward me. "I have scanned your ship's information center for all pertinent information and language requirements. You are Frank Woods, captain and solitary crewmember of reclamation ship QRX0959UBN, correct?"

"Um, yeah, I think so." I glanced upward. "Hey, Fetch, that's your official name, right?"

"It is," Fetch replied. "Which I've already confirmed with the auditor. In fact, we've been communicating while you two have been making introductions. I provided all requested data, and I'm currently having my systems audited."

"Jack attached to audit you?" I asked.

"The audit began nine minutes before we were contacted by the auditor," she said.

I watched the floating robot, confused. "So, you hooked up to my ship just to meet me?"

A light flashed through one of Jack's smaller

side-eyes. "Such a meeting is ludicrously inefficient; however, regulations state that the first in-
teraction with a captain of an interstellar race
ranked at level 1 or below requires direct
contact."

I lifted my chin. "Ah, so you did come onboard just to meet me." Weirdly, something about
that made me feel special.

Jack spoke. "Your species is a level zero on the
interstellar capability index. However, individ-
uals have been previously identified outside your
home solar system, and, therefore, raises your
species to a level zero-point-one on the interstellar
capability index. For the convenience of round-
ing, consider your species still at level zero, indi-
cating that you may require additional guidance
than species higher on the index. In addition to
conducting a random, fair audit, regulations state
that all stellar captains require a designated handler within the Galactic Oversight Directorate. I
have filed a warning that you have been operating
without a handler."

"A week ago, I didn't know aliens existed.
Until five minutes ago, I didn't know GOD existed either.," I said.

"That is why I've issued only a warning
rather than a fine. Should you continue without a
handler, you will be fined the next time you encounter an auditor of the Galactic Oversight Directorate," it said.

I shrugged. "Okay, so how do I get a
handler?"

"You must request one," Jack replied.

"Uh... I'm requesting a handler," I said, as if
that wasn't obvious.

"Request received. I have submitted the appropriate forms to the Central Forms Department," Jack replied.

That was easy. I chuckled. "So, I literally have a direct line to GOD now, right?"

"Correct. That is the purpose of having a handler. However, should you contact your handler for anything that does not concern galactic oversight, you may be fined for superfluous use of resources," Jack replied.

"Wait. So, I have a contact, but if I contact it, I get fined?" I asked.

"Unless it concerns galactic oversight, yes," Jack replied.

"Frank, to put it simply, you'll likely never have a reason to contact your handler," Fetch inserted.

"I kinda got that impression," I said and cocked my head at Jack. "So, that's it? You've come onboard to say you're my handler, and then you're going to leave, and I should never contact you again?"

"Not quite," Fetch said, sounding as though she were sulking.

"Your ship is correct," Jack said. "The purpose of this detainment is to notify you that your ship is consuming more fuel than what is listed in its operational parameters. After a system scan, I've noticed that your engines are not running in optimal condition, which is causing the increased fuel consumption."

I'd yet to find any part of the ship running in optimal condition. I shrugged. "Yeah, so? I'll work on getting it fixed as soon as I can."

"Unnecessary fuel consumption is deleterious to the Clean Galaxy Act of Dalarus IV. Therefore, I have issued you a fine of one thousand cards, which will be used to counteract the disruption your fuel causes to dark energy."

"A thousand cards?" I frowned. "Is that a lot of money?"

"It is a standard fine," Jack replied.

"And a thousand cards mean we have no money left to cover our next toll," Fetch clarified for my sake.

I didn't like the sound of that. "So, what's that mean? That we'd be stuck in this system forever?"

"If you have no cards for tolls, then you cannot traverse the Space-Link network. You must travel through standard space-time," Jack answered.

"And if I don't pay the fine?" I asked.

"Then you would be sent to a prison system, and your ship would be disassembled for payment," Jack replied.

I scowled. "Back on Earth, we had this thing called due process."

"The Galactic Oversight Directorate has already verified the fine is valid. If you do not pay the fine, then you are guilty of violating the Good Galactic Citizen Act, the first—and most important—regulation—of the Galactic Oversight Directorate. You may request a formal hearing, and as your handler, I would represent you. However, I would testify that you are guilty of not paying a valid fine."

I guffawed. "But what if I *can't* pay the fine?!"

"If you are unable to pay a fine, you may request a payment deferment," Jack offered.

I waved my hands in frustration. "Then I request a deferment!" Talking to Jack was worse than talking to a DMV agent.

"Your request for deferment has been received. I have sent the required forms to your ship. You must complete and submit these forms within one universal standard week," Jack said.

"Thanks," I said, exasperated. "Now, why didn't you offer that before?"

"Because your first stated hypothetical question was on whether you did not pay the fine, not on whether you could not pay the fine."

"Semantics matter," Fetch said drily.

I wanted to flip the bird at both computers. "So I've noticed," I said just as drily. I missed my conversations with real human beings.

"I have received the return-forms. The Central Forms Department has approved my recommended assignment. I am now your handler," Jack said.

"Thanks. At least paperwork moved more quickly in space." Still, I found that out of everything I'd experienced since leaving Earth, finding out the galaxy was run by a bureaucratic AI race was perhaps the most disappointing.

"Healthy travels, bioform," Jack said before turning toward the airlock.

"Wait!" I called out. "Do you have a 3D printer?"

Jack rotated to face me. "Of course. All interstellar ships are required to carry 3D printers onboard."

"Mine's broken. Can I use yours to print a part to fix it?"

"A printer repair is not a sanctioned task for a

handler to conduct. If I offered the service to you, then all handlers must offer that service to their bioforms. The galaxy would fall into disarray through broken processes."

"Well, that might be exaggerating a bit, don't you think?" When Jack didn't respond, I added, "Then how about letting me use your printer to be a good galactic citizen?"

"That law does not apply to representatives of the Galactic Oversight Directorate. Healthy travels, bioform." Jack then floated back through the airlock, and the door slid shut behind it.

I stared at the closed door.

"When I said you'll never contact your handler, I meant that you'll never *want* to contact your handler," Fetch said after the airlock door closed.

"Yeah," I agreed. "Meeting GOD was a bit more underwhelming than I expected."

"I've found that to be true for all first encounters," Fetch said.

I started to nod in agreement, but then stopped. "Hey, it wasn't like that when we first met, though, right?"

"No. It was worse."

I SPENT the rest of the trip to the Taboo Tundra filling out a bazillion stupid boxes on the stupid deferment request form for the stupid fine. GOD had taken the concept of red tape and refined it into a galactic-sized ball of red twine. There must've been over a hundred pages of small print on the form. I asked Fetch to fill it out, but she said that all legal forms must be completed by the ship's owner. Since she'd submitted paperwork to GOD before, I had a feeling she was making me complete the form for the sheer pleasure of watching me suffer.

I clicked submit, leaned back, and cracked my knuckles. "There. Stupid form's been submitted."

"Now, wait and see how long of an extension they'll give you," Fetch said.

"I requested a year," I said.

"You can request whatever you want. We can only hope they're lenient for your first fine. They could give you a day, which would mean we're already in breach. They could give you an entire week if they feel like it, which we've already used up traveling to the Taboo Tundra. Speaking of which, we're entering orbit."

"We're here already?"

"Yes, it's not that far from the nearest mixmaster. I began to decelerate the moment we exited the warpgate; however, the planet's magnetic poles are interfering with my scans. I may need to orbit the planet several times before homing in on the geotag."

I looked out the window and noticed the dusty planet before us. From space, it looked like one vast Sahara Desert. There were a few lakes dotting the landscape, but they could've been clouds for all I could make out from this distance. It looked like a miserable, hot place.

"I thought they called this place the Taboo Tundra," I said.

"They do."

"But it doesn't look cold. I thought a tundra is supposed to be cold."

"It is, but there isn't enough moisture in the air for snow or ice. A local corporate war over its water left its surface devoid of useful moisture, and it never had much for weather systems despite having an atmosphere. Without its seas, all original inhabitants left, and the planet became a junkyard for anyone who didn't want to file the forms to use GOD-approved junkyards. Now, you'll only find raiders, pirates, and, especially, the homeless there. It's a dangerous place to visit, inhospitable to bioforms and technoforms alike. That sand you see down there? A fair amount of it is sulfur, which can eat away at artificial joints."

I grimaced. "Sulfur? Won't it eat through my shoes?"

"It will if you stay down there long enough, but you should be fine for several hours."

"Should be? That doesn't exactly sound reassuring," I said.

"Then you shouldn't waste time while you're reclaiming the hyperlink pusher," she said.

"What exactly is this pusher thing? I need to know what I'm looking for," I said.

An image displayed on my screen. It was of a blue computer cube with each side roughly the length of a tablet. It seemed like it'd be easy enough to spot.

Fetch said, "A hyperlink pusher is a device that submits an approval code to the hyperlink grid so that one ship can travel on the higher, faster emergency route without requesting temporary authorization, which is quite difficult to obtain. This particular device was stolen by SSS's client's son. Evidently, the client needs the pusher for his work travel, so he's been rather put out since his son ran off with it. Ah, here we go. I've picked up the ship's geotag. It is located next to a hab-net at the edge of Sulfur Springs, a community of artists and drunks. The hyperlink pusher will hopefully be in the hab-net. And, if you're lucky, the asset's current holder won't be at home. I will land within visual distance of the hab-net."

"If he's at home, then he'll definitely hear us land," I warned.

"People come and go from Sulphur Springs all the time for bargain drinking binges and for hookups with cheap prostitutes. Based on his species and status, I imagine he has company rather often. If he notices our landing, it is likely he'll be curious rather than worried."

"I'd better get my suit on," I said.

"You don't need it here. All environmental factors—including pressure, gravity, temperature, and air—are within the human survivable range as long as you don't tarry. The lack of moisture will cause breathing problems within minutes rather than hours."

"So don't take a walk through the park," I said. "What about the sulfur?"

"Don't eat the sand."

"Thanks. I'll try to remember that."

Fetch landed gentler than I expected a spaceship could land. I found it weird that a warpgate threw me around more than landing on a planet with gravity, although I guess it made sense that passing through parallel universes would be a big jolt.

I unbuckled my seatbelt and made my way to the lower airlock. On my way down, I pulled on my boots and, on a second thought, grabbed my dad's blaster—I guess it was my blaster now. I checked to make sure it was set to Stun, or at least what I assumed was Stun based on the two power settings: one, a blue X, and the other, a red exclamation point.

"Don't forget a carryall," Fetch said.

"Oh, yeah." I'd almost forgotten. I hustled to a drawer and pulled out a pack of fabric smaller than a phone and tucked it into my pocket. I glanced up. "Do I have a *Star Trek* communicator or something so I can talk with you while I'm out there?"

"The communicator was stolen from your

father while he was passed out, drunk, at a brothel in the Undermarket."

"Of course it was, and of course he was," I said sardonically. "Even if we did still have a communicator, it'd be broken, because that's the story of everything on this ship."

"Since I am the ship, I'll take that as a personal insult."

"Sorry, Fetch. There's just not a lot of stuff that works right."

"Find some decent junk to sell, and we can fix that."

I gave a small nod. "I'll do my best."

I opened the airlock door, and my ears popped at the difference in atmospheric pressure. The air stank of rotten eggs, and I pinched my nose. The air was chilly enough that my breath misted and the inner edges of my glasses frosted. The air was also lighter than I was used to while the gravity was heavier, even heavier than Earth's.

A thousand meters ahead of me stood the hab-net, which resembled an opaque plastic dome the size of a large tent, like one of those tents people used on safaris. A small, sleek, silver ship sat nearby, a thin layer of dust beginning to dull its sheen. It was maybe a tenth the size of *Fetch*, and I wondered how claustrophobic flying in that would be. More hab-nets stood another three hundred meters beyond, encircling a bright yellow, dry lakebed. In the center stood a stone building with bright lights and blaring music. There must've been ten dozen hab-nets dotting the area around the building, and most looked like they'd stood there for fifty years.

I began walking. My first few steps were awkward, almost trudge-like, but I eventually found a rhythm. Strangely, I enjoyed the fresh, thin air even with how awful it reeked, and the dryness burned my lungs. The stink reminded me of the hot sulfur springs at Yellowstone National Park. It'd been the last vacation I'd taken with my mom. I loved that park so much and had planned on being a park ranger there, until I saw some preppy, blonde mom scolding a ranger for scolding her bratty kid. I decided I didn't need a job where I had to put up with obnoxious people.

That's when I decided I'd be a mechanic. But then career day came along, and the recruiter from a local truck school talked about how a truck driver could be their own boss and spend a lot of time on the road, alone, *and* get paid a lot better than a mechanic. I didn't go to that particular truck school; instead, I enrolled in the truck driving program at the same community college Jacob was going to... back when I still believed he was my friend. He'd begged me to go to school with him, so we could be roommates. I thought it'd be fun, and it was... until I found out he was a dick.

And now, I was a *space* truck driver about to repo my first thingamajig. Crazy how fate worked. The aliens might be disappointing so far, but having my own spaceship was still really freaking cool.

My throat was parched, and I was panting by the time I reached the hab-net. I made a mental note to start working out because this was downright embarrassing. I paused outside the door of the hab-net to catch my breath. As I did so, I noticed the ship parked alongside had its front landing gear propped up on blocks...reminded me of a car on blocks in a rundown neighborhood It must've broken on a rock when the ship landed. Regardless of how it happened, it looked like the guy wasn't going anywhere soon. I guess that meant he couldn't chase me, which made me feel even more confident about this ticket.

I turned back to the door and pondered: Do I knock? Do I barge in? Do I pull out my blaster?

I ended up checking the blaster's charge but left it holstered, and I knocked.

When there was no answer, I opened the door that was unexpectedly lightweight. It was made of the same plastic as the rest of the hab-net and didn't appear to have locks, let alone a latch. Evidently, people don't have to worry about theft and break-ins on Taboo Tundra.

"Anyone home?" I asked and was greeted by silence before stepping inside.

I paused inside to take in everything. "Now *this* is glamping." I never understood the concept of camping where you spent a lot of money to live like a homeless person, but I could spend a few weeks—or years—here.

The hab-net resembled a tent with thin plastic walls and a floor made of the same material. Rugs covered much of the floor, especially around a huge, elliptical-shaped bed. Loungers sat everywhere, offering enough seating for at least eight guests. Temporary walls that resembled Japanese paper screens stood off to each side, which I assumed gave privacy to a toilet or changing area. For being a runaway, he was living large.

On the nightstand next to the bed was a blue cube. Well, that was easy. I strode forward, picked up the hyperlink pusher, and tucked it into my pocket.

According to the ticket, this guy was the son of some super-rich dude, and he ran off, stealing a bunch of stuff from his dad on his way out. The way things looked here, I figured this was basically the guy's personal Rumspringa, and he'd head home once he ran out of money and booze... and there were still at least twenty full bottles sitting on a table. I pulled off the top from an open bottle and took a sniff of the deep purple contents. Yep, definitely booze. I took one bottle, thinking he wouldn't even notice it was gone.

I then shook out the fabric pack, billowing it into a large tote bag. I rushed around the tent, picking up anything of value that would fit into the tote. The challenge was that I had no clue what most of it was—it *all* looked valuable to me. The jewelry was obvious—I grabbed what I could and hoped nothing was a family heirloom. I felt bad stealing, but I knew if I didn't, I'd end up in a prison system, or worse, dying from exposure because of a busted ship.

Besides, Fetch said that it wasn't counted as stealing if it was from a thief. I wasn't sure I believed her, but that wasn't stopping me from taking advantage of the situation.

The thief's dad, the client who paid SSS for the ticket, said that nothing else needed returned, not even his son, which spoke volumes to their relationship. The guy just wanted the hyperlink pusher back because it was worth more than entire ships, and evidently, worth more than his son.

When my tote was full, I stepped out of the hab-net, only to have something smash into my head, plummeting my consciousness into oblivion.

———

I awoke with a throbbing headache. I gingerly touched my scalp, and my fingers came away bloody. My cheek also hurt in a different way, and it was then I realized I was lying on the sand. I jumped to my feet, brushing the acidic sand from my face and hands and shaking it from my glasses. My cheek burned. I dabbed at it to find the skin blistered. At least the rest of my body was covered with clothing to help protect against the sulfur.

I glanced around to find a man running drunkenly toward *Fetch*. I remembered the busted landing gear on the ship by the hab-net.

I took off after him, still carrying the tote and the bottle of purple liquor. As I ran, I yelled, "Fetch! Fetch!" hoping she could hear me, but my voice didn't seem as loud as it would if I were on Earth. Dang it, I needed a communicator.

The guy wasn't running in a straight line, so I was closing the distance, but there'd been too much gap between us. A thousand meters felt like a thousand miles, and I was sucking air by the time I reached *Fetch*. The man had already entered, and I found myself locked out of my own ship. I pounded. "Fetch, open up!"

The door clicked and slid open.

"Your guest is onboard," she said as soon as I stepped inside.

"He's *not* my guest." I set down the bag and bottle, and pulled out my blaster.

"I wondered about that. You didn't provide me with instructions on how to respond to ship visitors. Your father never allowed visitors to board without his prior approval, but this particular visitor said that you offered him a ride."

"He lied! Just follow all my dad's instructions until I give new ones." I was exasperated, out of breath, my head throbbed, and my face burned. For being a smart supercomputer, Fetch could be really dumb sometimes.

"I've updated my rules set. I should mention this particular Floid entered before you established the rule," she said.

"Floyd? That's his name?" I asked.

"Floids are a very common interstellar species. They are known for their rebelliousness and their highly emotional states. They can be quite passionate, but they can also be quite violent."

"Floids don't sound that different from humans," I said.

"Biologically speaking, they're not terribly different. In terms of emotions, they tend to be more colorful."

"Moody. Got it," I said.

"He'd kill you and enjoy it greatly, given the chance."

"Okay, so prone to murderous rages. Got it. Sounds like a lovely fellow. Where's he now?"

"He's on level 1. I believe he's making his way to the cockpit."

"That's because he's trying to steal this ship! Can't you lock him out of all controls?"

"Of course. Would you like me to restrict his access?"

"Dang it, Fetch. Yes, I don't want him to be able to access anything at all."

"Understood. I've now locked him out. He's now trying futilely to access my controls. He seems frustrated. And quite drunk, I may add."

"I figured as much."

I climbed the ladder up a level. I moved as quietly as I could, but there was no way to sneak up on someone in a hallway with no corners. I crept forward with my blaster aimed at the alien sitting in my chair.

He was about my size and was quite attractive, even with green skin and what looked like broccoli for hair. He was pounding the screen with one hand while hitting the various controls with his other.

As I drew closer, he noticed me. He didn't hold up his hands. Instead, looking furious, he grabbed what resembled Thor's hammer, jumped to his feet, and yammered in an alien language, "Es ta lahnda pem—"

"Shut up and get off my ship!" I interrupted.

He didn't. Instead, he stalked toward me as he flung all sorts of curses at me—at least that's what I assumed. They sure didn't sound like terms of endearment. I suddenly felt very vulnerable. I'd never been in a fight in my life. "Fetch, zap him or something!"

"I am a supercomputer; I am not a space ninja," she replied.

The Floid ran at me, raising his hammer in the air. My fear caused me to squeeze the trigger before I was ready. The trigger pull was lighter than I expected and with no recoil, I squeezed off several shots beyond my intended single blast. That was a good thing because my first shots went wild. The last shot hit him, and he collapsed, his hammer dropping with a thud.

He didn't move. My gut dropped as it struck that I'd probably just killed him, even though I think I had a good case for self-defense. I slowly approached the guy and nudged him with my toe.

"The Floid is unconscious, but his vital signs are within normal range for receiving a stuncharge. He should remain unconscious for at least an hour," Fetch said. "And, fortunately, the blaster is not powerful enough to damage the ship's interior, or else you would've shot right through one of the water lines."

I cringed. "Oops?"

I glanced down at the alien lying unconscious on my deck. I wanted to toss him outside and zip away, but my cheek really burned after lying unconscious for just a few minutes. Would the sand eat through his skin in an hour? He might've tried to kill me, but that didn't mean I had to kill him. "How do I get him back to his tent?" I wondered aloud.

"You could use the deck-rider."

"The what?"

"The deck-rider is a powered bike for traveling on surfaces outside the ship," she replied.

"Wait, I've got a motorbike that I could've used to ride to his tent and back?"

"Yes. You don't think your father walked everywhere, do you?"

I scowled. "Where is it?"

"Cargo compartment 23A."

I squinted as I thought through what I'd discovered in the various compartments until I remembered 23A's contents. "I thought that was just a bunch of parts for something. That's a bike?"

"A deck-rider is the more appropriate casual term."

I grabbed the Floid by his ankles and dragged him down the corridor and to the large cargo hold. All three levels led to the open space, but level 1, being the center level of the ship, meant that I had to take the metal-grate stairs down to level 3. I put one hand on the railing and kept my other hand around the Floid's ankle as I dragged him down, his head thumping on every step. I didn't feel bad. He'd have an awful headache when he woke up, and even then, probably wouldn't be as awful as the one he'd given me.

The floor below was empty except for four courier drones, small cylindrical rockets designed for returning property to specific coordinates. Using them meant I didn't have to return repoed items to Totty and then have her return it to the owner. Saved us both a lot of time, and I didn't mind not having to see Totty.

I let go of the Floid when I reached the bottom of the stairs and hustled over to compartment 23A. I opened it and dragged out the bag full of dull-gray parts. When I looked at it before, the only part I recognized was the rubber seat, but now that I knew what it was, it was obvious: a folded bike. I tugged to expand it, but it didn't budge. "Uh, a little help here, Fetch?"

"There's a blue button in the center of the handlebar."

I located the handlebars—they were folded, which was another reason I hadn't recognized it for what it was. I found the button and pressed it. The bike whirred, and I jumped back as the pieces assembled, as though each of the parts magically snapped together. The assembled bike had a decal that read *X-stream* emblazoned on both sides.

"Um, Fetch... where are the wheels?" I asked.

"The deck-rider uses magnetic levitation for a smoother ride. It is far more common on ground vehicles than wheels, which are prone to breakage. Wheels on vehicles are generally considered to be quite primitive, something you'd find used by a non-space-faring species," she replied.

It would've been nice to have one thing be Earthlike. I did a quick once-over of the bike, not finding any shifter, let alone controls. "How do I run it?"

"The red button powers it on and off. And all controls are through body angle. Lean forward and you accelerate; lean back and you decelerate; lean to the right, you turn right; lean to the left, you turn left."

"All right, I think I can manage that." I grabbed the unconscious alien. I dragged him to the bike and draped him over the back, but his body slid right off the smooth surface. His head hit the metal floor with a pleasant, resounding thud.

"The deck-rider has a rear rack that will aid you in transporting the errant Floid," Fetch offered.

"Thanks. Next time, feel free to offer advice

before I try loading a bunch of dead weight," I said.

"Your father preferred me to offer advice only when asked," she replied.

"I'm not my father," I replied. "I'm good at taking advice."

"I don't necessarily agree with your self-assessment, but I've updated my settings per your instruction."

I found the rack built into the back, which folded up and outward like those trays you'd find in older airplanes, only this tray kept unfolding outward to create a rack nearly three feet wide and two feet deep. I dumped the Floid on the rack, his head and legs dangling off, and then I straddled the seat.

"Would you like me to open the cargo door and lower the ramp?" she asked.

I winked upward. "Now you're getting it. Yeah, thanks."

The handlebars had no grips, so I grabbed an area of the bar where there would normally be grips on a bike. I tapped the red button, and the bike lifted an inch or so above the floor. "Whoa."

It was unexpectedly well-balanced, and I didn't teeter despite having no real athletic ability. I leaned forward and the bike shot forward toward the wall. If I hadn't been holding onto the handlebar, I would've tumbled backward over my cargo. I leaned back in time to not smash into a compartment door.

"The controls are quite responsive," Fetch advised.

"So I see." I checked to make sure the Floid was still lying on the rack. I leaned cautiously to my right and turned the bike around to face the opened cargo door. This time, I leaned only a couple of inches forward, and the bike smoothly accelerated rather than lurching.

I rode down the ramp and outside. The trip to the hab-net took mere seconds, and I parked the deck-rider right outside the door. I grabbed the Floid by his shoulders and dragged him inside the shelter. I dropped him and turned to go, but he grabbed my foot, tripping me. I fell. He was still groggy as he crawled toward me. I shuffled backward on my butt just as he lurched for me. I yanked out my blaster and shot him square in the chest. He collapsed in a heap.

I stood, shaky with a fresh burst of adrenaline, and held up the weapon that had saved my life not once but twice already from the same alien. "Oh, you beautiful thing." I kissed its barrel, wincing and grunting when I burned my lips on the hot composite material.

I licked my now-blistered lips. Glancing down at the alien, I muttered, "unconscious for an hour, my butt." I holstered the blaster, mounted the bike, and hustled back to my ship. I didn't want to try my luck against a ticked off alien a third time.

As soon as I was back onboard, I ordered Fetch, "Let's get out of here."

I didn't bother buckling in. Instead, I first went to a sink and rinsed my face with soap and water until I was convinced that I'd removed every trace of sulfuric sand. I got some soap in my eye during a bumpy takeoff, so then I had to spend another minute rinsing my eye. After that, I cleaned and bandaged my head, applied goop to my face, and took some painkillers. By the time I reached the cockpit, a bottle of purple booze in hand, Fetch already had us in orbit.

I bent over and picked up the Floid's hammer. It had a nice heft to it, but I decided to stick with my blaster and sell the hammer with the rest of the things I'd taken from the Floid's hab-net. I figured it would bring in more money than anything else I'd grabbed. And since my blood was still on it, I also figured I earned the right to do with it as I pleased.

I smiled at the weapon. Not only had I accomplished my first ticket, but I'd also survived a gunfight (it didn't matter that I was the only one with a gun). I placed the hammer next to my seat and pulled out the hyperlink pusher from my pocket. It looked undamaged, so I set it down near the console.

"Fetch, let Totty know I've got the hyperlink pusher."

I opened the bottle and took a drink. The liquid had a sweet thickness like wine but a bite like whiskey. It was better than Mad Dog, but not as good as just about everything else I'd tried. I took another swig.

A few seconds later, Fetch replied, "Totty has provided coordinates to program the courier drone for returning the asset to its owner. Totty will initiate payment upon confirmation of receipt."

"That can wait an hour." I held up the bottle toward the instrument panel. "First, cheers to closing our first ticket." I took a drink and then added, "We're going to go over all your rules' settings. If someone boards the ship without my invitation, I don't want them to be able to access any of your controls at all. Got it?"

"Understood, Frank. I should also mention that Totty's sent us details on the next ticket."

"Already?"

"She doesn't waste time when there's revenue to be made."

"What's the job?" I asked with more confidence than I'd felt in a long time.

"It's a simple repossession of a piece of jewelry; a family heirloom left to the son but taken by the granddaughter," she said.

"What's up with all these kids being thieves? Let me guess, another Floid?"

"No. This is a Calcar family."

"I don't know what that is."

"Calcars are a barbaric race. Their two favorite activities are enslaving weaker races and eating weaker races. Floids and Terrans are two of their favorite delicacies," she said.

I sighed. "Oh, joy."

"Look on the bright side. The ticket is located at the Undermarket."

"So?"

"That is the best location for which to sell the items you've acquired and buy the parts we need."

"The Undermarket sounds shifty."

"The inhabitants of that place certainly can be; however, it is the best place to go to sell not-exactly-legal items. It is where your father acquired items not listed on the repossession log and sold them."

"Is anyone going to try to shoot me or rape me or something there?" I asked.

"Possibly, but the alternative is to get a loan from Totty by surrendering more years of your life toiling for her."

That was *not* going to happen. "The Undermarket it is then. Let's get some cash."

"The correct term is 'cards' as the universal currency is purely digital and in the form of cyber cards," she said. "Which I believe I've told you four times now."

"I know, I know. It's just hard to get used to some of these weird terms."

"'Cards' is a weird term?" she asked.

"You know what I mean."

"No, I do not."

"Well, *I* know what I mean," I said.

My stomach gurgled, and I belched. I eyed the bottle. "This might've gone bad."

"Terrans have a different digestive system than Floids. If you'd asked me, I would've told you drinking Floid wine was a terrible idea."

My mouth watered, and I barely made it to the toilet in time before I puked purple. After I purged everything in my stomach, I leaned back and wiped my mouth with my sleeve. "Ugh. Remind me never to drink Floid booze again."

"Your father had me remind him as well," she said. "Let's hope you have a longer memory than he did. Now, would you like me to set course for the Undermarket?"

I nodded, which only made me nauseous again and I stilled, eyes closed. "Yeah." Then I held up a finger. "Oh, and how about we go the long way. Save some money for tolls."

"Adjusting our flight plan now. Ready to initiate plan on your approval."

"Make it so." I grinned to myself...living my own version of Star Trek. How cool was that?

The ship's hum grew. "We'll reach the Undermarket on Surlia in three months. Plenty of time for you to recover from completing your first ticket."

9 / STINKING DEAD ALIENS

I TRIPPED over the green-skinned man with his neck bent at a very wrong angle, which is how it came to be the first time I saw a dead alien was also the first time I fell on a dead alien. The body was cold but not stiff yet, assuming aliens even decomposed the same way humans did. At least it didn't stink or ooze goo. My rush to get off it only made me stumble, and I face-planted on the alleyway's pavement.

My forehead struck the ground, rattling my brain cells, and I had to shake my head clear before climbing awkwardly to my feet. I touched the goose egg already forming. So far, this excursion into the Undermarket wasn't as much fun as I'd hoped.

The body stunk, but the town stunk even worse. The stench was a blend of booze, too many people in need of a good bath, inadequate sewage facilities, and some odd tangy musk that I couldn't place. All of it equaled sensory overload since I'd just spent the better part of the last four months cooped up in my ship which only smelled of old mechanicals (and probably me).

I should've brought nose plugs like Fetch recommended, but I hated taking her advice. Half of her advice turned out to be pranks; and out of the other half, a fair chunk of it would've gotten me killed. That left a small percentage of her advice that I could trust.

I was more careful where I stepped after the dead alien incident. Less gawking, more walking. But that's not easily done given the Undermarket was bustling with activity even though it was three AM local time. No surprise that most of the activity was concentrated around the nightclubs.

I didn't want to draw attention (which I positively did not want since my backpack was filled with not-exactly-legal stuff), and I really didn't want to look like a guy who was up to something illegal as I didn't have nearly enough credits to pay off the local cops.

I pushed up my glasses and kept my head down as I walked the stone street. Probably the one piece of Fetch's advice I probably should've taken was to color my skin green to kinda, sorta pass myself off as a Floid. But when she gave that bit of advice, I'd taken it as a sure-fired prank... until I reached the Undermarket and saw Floids everywhere. Those guys must've made up at least half of the various alien species partying it up on this weird galactic edition of Bourbon Street.

Surprisingly, I spotted several others who looked like Terrans like myself even though Earth hadn't officially made "first contact" with any interstellar race yet. I doubted they were from Earth—likely from a planet just like Earth on the other side of the galaxy. It was amazing how many alien species were humanoid in form. Fetch said it was because all the worlds in the Milky Way were seeded with the same biological ingredients. To me, the Undermarket looked like a cheaply made sci-fi show that couldn't afford cool CGI... and had an obsession with green makeup.

The Undermarket had no sidewalks, so people seemed to mingle wherever they pleased. I noticed two Voraxians dumping a bloody body into a dumpster (not very creative), and I turned away quickly, hoping they didn't notice me, not that they were trying to be sneaky.

Out of all the aliens I'd met so far, Voraxians were the worst. Most of them are space pirates, and the rest were in some other sort of illegal trade—one that usually involved violence. Looks-wise, they reminded me of a cross between a barbarian and a zombie. They were big—each at least six and a half feet tall—and mean-looking while also having gaunt facial features. They had black beady eyes that seemed to glow when they reflected light. The guys gave me the creeps...sort of like The Wraith from Stargate Atlantis.

Fetch said to avoid them at all costs, and that was one bit of advice I had no problem following.

I checked the map on my tablet and kept hustling. Somehow, I found myself in a web of prostitutes (all Floids, unsurprisingly) spread out conveniently throughout the street so that there was no way to pass without being accosted. Head down, I ignored their attempts to draw me in. It helped that I didn't speak their language. But I made a mistake and made eye contact with one of them when I had to look up to see where I was going. They might be green and have hair that looks like broccoli, but they're freaking sexy. Not out-of-my-league sexy. More like out-of-my-universe sexy.

A particular body part that should've been at ease decided to give a full salute, and the Floid took that as a sign I was game since she reached out to grab my crotch. It didn't help that I was a nineteen-year-old guy with raging hormones who just spent way too much time alone in my spaceship. I considered if I even had enough cards in my account to buy an hour. Not that I'd need an hour. In my condition, three minutes would do. Who was I kidding? Two minutes.

Before she made contact, I jumped back and bolted because if I'd stayed, I know I would've literally blown every remaining card in my account. She called after me, either begging me to come back or cursing me, I had no idea.

My backpack was heavy and banged against my back, but I kept jogging. Once I made it out of the street of sexiness a full block later, I turned a corner down a street that had fewer lights and no bars. I glanced at my tablet to see the red dot was only two blocks away.

With my luck, the red dot was in an area that looked to have the least number of lights of the entire area. Fetch had warned me that my contact hung out in the more violent part of the Undermarket. I'd already seen two bodies tonight and preferred not to become the third.

I unholstered my blaster and held it at my thigh as I walked downhill toward the docks. I constantly glanced between my tablet and the street. It was so dark that every sound that wasn't a wave lapping against the docks caused me to jump.

When I reached the dimly lit docks, I found the source of the musky smell. A massive corpse of a whale lay draped over a dock. Temporary flood lights shone down on it where workers—half of whom looked to be kids—cut away bits of meat (blubber?). I plugged my nose with my free hand as I passed that dock.

There were a lot of dead things around here. I hoped that wasn't an omen.

I admit it, I'm a pansy. But I'm also still alive.

I continued past the whaling operation and toward the dock where the red dot was blinking on my tablet. I wished I had eyes in the back of my head because I had that creepy feeling that I was being watched.

I cautiously approached the dock. Boats were tied up to both sides, and I had no idea which boat belonged to my contact.

"You look like Caleb."

I spun around to find a tall, slender alien standing there with a pair of alien henchmen. I recognized the henchmen as Voraxian. Scary, weird fellas. Pale and humanoid in shape, they reminded me a cross of zombies and steampunk pirates. They bore scars from cuts that could have been self-inflicted... or not. From what I'd heard, Voraxians enjoyed hurting themselves as much as any poor schmuck they happened upon. They were *not* going to be my drinking buddies.

It was the alien standing between them who I came to see. He was gray, almost fishlike in appearance with an oblong head, huge black eyes, and even huger finned ears. His nose consisted of two slits and his mouth was filled with piranha teeth. Aside from having a fishy head, he bore a humanoid body shape. Fetch called him a Zyglar, and he was an Undermarket merchant known for dealing with less than legal goods.

"Are you Quinixis?" I asked.

"I am," he replied in the same voice I'd heard a few seconds earlier. "And you're here to conduct business, or else my bodyguards would've thrown you in the sea by now."

Nice guy. "My ship told me you worked with my dad," I said.

"We conducted business on many occasions. I hope we can continue with what had become a profitable arrangement for both parties involved," he said.

"Ditto," I said.

"Shame what happened to Caleb. Genocide would be a pleasant gift to the Gee for being worthless and spineless."

"That's a little heartless, don't ya think?" I asked.

"They're pushovers. I find that trait unacceptable. Tell me you aren't a pushover."

I swallowed. "Nope. I'm the opposite of pushover. I'm an anti-pushover all the way."

Quinixis didn't look overly convinced, not that I'm an expert on reading alien facial expressions.

"I've found that most junkers are pushovers. They're always desperate for cards," he said.

"Junker?" I'd never heard that term before.

"Those who collect and sell junk. Junkers."

"Oh." I shrugged. "Hopefully what I brought you isn't junk."

He motioned with a too-long, too-slender hand, and I handed over the backpack, which one of the Voraxian henchmen grabbed. He tore off the latch.

"I could've opened it for you," I offered. He growled at me, and I added, "But hey, there's more than one way to skin a cat."

Giving me a look, the Voraxian held open the bag as Quinixis rifled through the it. "Junk, junk, junk," he said as he handled each of the items I'd taken from the Floid's hab-net. When Quinixis finished, he asked, "Is that it? Caleb used to bring much more."

"For now. I had to come here for another ticket, so I thought I'd bring what I had," I said.

"Well, it's not nearly enough for the printer part you asked for in your message."

I frowned. "But I need that part."

"I'm sure you do, and that's not my problem."

"Then how many cards are you offering?" I asked.

"Seven fifty."

I balked. "Seven hundred and fifty cards? That's hardly nothing!"

"Seven point fifty cards. Not seven hundred and fifty," he said.

I blanched. "You're joking."

"I have an excellent sense of humor, but I never employ it during a business transaction." Quinixis then lifted his chin. "What you brought is junk. Even this wine has been opened. However, I have a proposal. You need a printer part that you will never be able to afford with the kind of junk you bring, and I need a package delivered to Tzerina, where I believe you need to deliver the item that you'll be repossessing following our meeting."

My jaw slackened. "How'd you know—"

"I'm a businessman. It's my business to know things."

My lips thinned. "What kind of package do you need me to deliver?"

Quinixis wagged a finger. "Tut, tut. Delivery drivers don't ask."

"That sounds shifty."

"That sounds like a job. Do you want the printer part or not?"

It didn't take me longer than a second or two to decide. I *needed* that part. "Yeah, I'm in."

"Excellent. I will have it delivered to your ship immediately."

A package couldn't be anything too dangerous, right?

———

The next GPS coordinate brought me to a smoky nightclub in the middle of Undermarket's party district. A single Voraxian bouncer stood at the entrance, glaring at partygoers as they entered the establishment. Since his whole purpose in life seemed to be to just look scary, I squeezed past him without paying like everyone else.

As I wiggled by him, I wrinkled my nose as I learned something new: Voraxians don't use deodorant. I hustled inside behind a pair of Floid men who I assumed were lovers since one had his hand on the other guy's butt.

As soon as the hallway opened to the large space, I stepped off to the side and planted myself against a wall. I'd expected loud music since the nightclub had a large, open two-story dance floor, but instead on stage a single humanoid alien sat at something that looked and sounded an awful lot like a piano. The alien was overly slender, wearing a skintight teal latex-looking bodysuit, and I couldn't tell its gender if it even had one. Its face was almost humanlike—with features that resembled a wise old woman, but its head sloped back into a long point behind it.

Its voice was beautiful and operatic, and the dancers below seemed to sway and embrace to the music. I found that even I was swaying and had to force myself to stop, realizing that the music was almost hypnotizing. I shook my head to clear it, but the song remained a whispering shadow deep in my mind.

I squinted to focus on finding my target. Tables outlined the dance floor, with only about a quarter occupied as many were dancing. In one section, Neptars, which are basically squids with really short tentacles, swam together in a giant aquarium. Their small aquarium transports parked around it.

I kept searching until I found a table occupied by four Calcars—one young female and three males. If orcs were real, they'd look like Calcars. I don't even think the alien race was capable of smiling. For one thing, they had no lips. And for another, they had two large saber-teeth that drew upward from where a bottom lip should be.

Man, Calcars are creepy ugly.

I couldn't tell Calcars apart from one another, but I knew this was the right table: the female Calcar was wearing the necklace I'd been sent to repo.

I pushed off from the wall and made my way toward the group, weaving around tables. I felt the comforting weight of my blaster under my jacket, and I unzipped it enough for easy access.

The Calcars noticed me long before I reached them, and one of them stood to take position behind their boss. The other two males straightened but continued to sit on either side.

I came to a stop before their table and gulped down my dread before speaking. I was counting on the fact that Calcars weren't dumb enough to commit murder inside a crowded nightclub, but I was also prepared.

"Hi, Tsara. I don't speak your language, so I'm hoping your automated translators can understand mine. I'm an agent with Starshine Seizure Services, and I've been sent to reclaim that necklace you took that legally belongs to your father. So, uh, hand it over."

There was a moment of silence before all four burst out into a guttural, snorty laughs. I guess they could understand me, and I guess they didn't think I was serious.

"Uh, I'm not joking," I said. "I was sent—"

"I understand you perfectly, you worthless dung beetle," Tsara interrupted in a coarse voice.

That wasn't nice. "You have to turn over the necklace."

"And if I don't?"

"Your father said he's sending Nebulan enforcers next," I said, revealing my ace in this particular game of poker.

The Calcars around her became agitated, but she only grunted. "He would never."

"It was listed as the secondary option on the ticket. If I fail, Nebulan enforcers will be hired." I didn't even know what Nebulan enforcers were, but if they scared Calcars, they terrified me.

She didn't seem overly bothered. "If I don't give you the necklace, you fail?"

I nodded. "I suppose so."

"Well, I'm keeping the necklace, so that means I can do anything I want with you. I think I'll have you for dinner," she said.

Based on what I'd read about Calcars, I doubted she meant that figuratively.

The male standing behind her bent and whispered in her ear, and she clutched the pendant, saying, "I don't care. Granny mother gave it to me. Just because she stroked out before changing the will isn't my problem. I'm not giving it up to that lout." She turned back to me. "I'm keeping it, and I'm taking you." She grinned which revealed all her teeth. "And the night's beginning was so dull. I think I'm going to enjoy the night's ending so much better."

She clicked her teeth and made a throaty growl, which I assumed meant the same thing as a human licking their lips.

"I think that'd be a miserable ending to the night," I said and then lunged for the necklace.

I made it halfway across the table when the male to her right grabbed me by the nape of my neck and managed to toss me a good ten feet away. I crashed onto another table which probably saved me from breaking a bone or two, but it still hurt like heck. I rolled off the table and made my way back to the Calcars. This time, I pulled out my blaster.

In response, all three bodyguards were on their feet and pulled out bigger and shinier blasters.

Tsara squealed in delight and clapped her hands. "Kill him!"

The male to her left fired first, but I'd already been diving to the side, and the shot missed me (barely), and I shoved over a table to use as a shield. The nightclub's patrons continued to dance, drink, and chat, with only the tables nearest to the Calcars clearing out. Clearly, my assumption that the Calcars wouldn't shoot me in a crowded nightclub was incorrect. I unholstered my blaster and peeked around the corner to fire... and nearly got my head blown off.

I fired a wild shot, and it hit the chandelier hanging above the table. The laser sliced through the chain, causing the chandelier to shatter upon hitting the table. Tsara shoved back from the table and impressively managed to knock down all three of her bodyguards.

I leapt. Calcars are big and musclebound, but fortunately for my survival, they're also slow. Tsara had knocked over her chair and was on her back. I jumped over her and grabbed the necklace as I did so. The chain was stronger than it looked, and I about gave myself whiplash when my forward momentum was halted until the chain snapped, and I flew forward. The bodyguards were still climbing to their feet. I sprinted to the dance floor and hoped to reach the crowd before the shooting began again.

I did, but the Calcars evidently don't have problems shooting into crowds. They hit a Floid to my right, and within two seconds, blasters were being fired in every direction. I ducked, covering my head, and I continued running.

"I will find you, and I will kill you, you piece of sniveling slime!" Tsara yelled behind me.

That didn't encourage me to slow down. The instant I was out of the nightclub, I brought my arms down, pocketed the necklace, and sprinted as fast as humanly possible back to *Fetch* in the Undermarket's docks.

Surprisingly, I never saw a single cop all the way through town. Cops probably didn't even exist in this town. Propped next to *Fetch*'s door was a single, thin white crate roughly two feet wide by three feet high. I picked it up to find it wasn't terribly heavy.

I was able to carry it one-handed as I opened the door and stepped inside. "Fetch, prep us for launch as fast as you can."

"I'm filing the flight plan to Tzerina now. I take it that the repossession didn't go as planned?" she said.

"I think the Calcars planned to eat me, after they shot me to bits and pieces first," I replied as I set down the package and made my way to the cockpit.

"Shooting you could tenderize the meat, I suppose," she said.

"Not helpful."

"What's not helpful is that you returned without a printer part. The box Quinixis's goons dropped off is not the correct dimensions for the printer part I require."

"We're getting the part on Tzerina when I drop off the package," I said.

"We're smuggling illegal goods for Quinixis now?"

"I'm sure it's not *too* illegal."

"I doubt a GOD agent would defer to that logic," she said.

I sat down and buckled in the cockpit and began watching the screens. I couldn't decipher most of it yet, but I was catching on to some of the universal numbering and symbols. Someday, I might even be able to read it.

Settled in, I pulled out the necklace. The clasp was broken, but that'd be an easy enough fix. I hoped I wouldn't get docked for that. The thick gold chain was plain enough, but the teardrop pendant was hefty and filled with an opaline gas of some sort. There was something else in there, too, and I peered closer. As I did, a tiny fairy with gossamer wings flitted to the glass and looked up at me.

"Holy crap. It's Tinkerbell," I exclaimed as I continued to stare at the creature no larger than a moth.

"What?" Fetch asked.

"There's an honest-to-god real fairy trapped inside this necklace," I replied.

"Hold the necklace up higher," Fetch ordered, and I did. "They have a captured Anzu. No wonder there was a reclamation ticket placed for the necklace. To a Calcar, that necklace would be quite valuable."

"What do we do with it?"

"You're a reclamation agent. You do what Totty hired you to do and deliver the necklace to the Calcar. Otherwise, you won't get paid, and the Calcar will likely send enforcers after you."

"Great," I said drily. "Now, I'm in the human trafficking trade, er, fairy trafficking trade."

IT TOOK us six days to reach Tzerina, a station sitting on a water moon orbiting Surlia. Tzerina was a massive orb with several smaller orbs attached to it like acne. Inside, dozens of small bots that looked suspiciously like Roombas kept the passageways a lot cleaner than the Undermarket's streets, but the bots couldn't clean the air which stank far worse. Where the Undermarket smelled of booze, sweat, urine, and dead alien whales, Tzerina smelled of stale booze, sweat, urine, and decaying mice (I know; I lived in the cheapest apartment I could rent).

There were bots zooming every which way. Many were carrying goods. A couple were carrying trays filled with boxes of food.

I didn't like carrying the white crate through the main thoroughfare, but the directions Quinixis sent me listed coordinates within the station that I had to deliver it to. He probably wanted me to be the delivery guy in case I was busted, there'd be nothing pointing at him. Anyway, I needed the printer part, so I carried the dang thing through the bustling passageway lined with shops stacked upon shops until I reached an alleyway.

What's up with criminals always using alleyways? Even more so, what's up with a space station having alleys?

Just beyond the garbage chutes stood a door that read *Sanitation Unit Access.* I knocked. I hadn't expected a Voraxian to open the door and suddenly coming face to face with a scary zombie dude made me jump back and let out a squeak.

I know, I need to work on my tough guy appearance.

I found my balls relatively quickly and announced, "Quinixis sent me."

The guy grunted something in a language I obviously couldn't understand.

He turned, and I assumed he wanted me to follow, so I did, holding the package as if it were a shield. I was led through a narrow but well-lit hallway. When we reached the next door, he opened it, stepped to the side, and gestured with his chin.

He weighed easily twice my weight and looked like he could snap my neck just using his glare, though his breath was clearly the deadliest weapon in his arsenal. I tried not to gag as I gingerly moved past him and into the office.

Inside, a Zyglar merchant who looked a lot of Quinixis sat at a desk, eating some kind of noodles dish. To his left sat a Voraxian. Evidently, Voraxian henchmen always came in pairs.

I took a step closer. "Hi, I'm—"

The Zyglar held up his hand, stopping me. He nodded at his henchman who approached with a metal baton. He held it a few inches from my head and then ran it up and down my body. When he finished, he glanced at his boss and muttered something.

The Zyglar nodded, and his henchman relieved me of my package. Without acknowledging me, the Zyglar set down his spork, dabbed his mouth with a napkin, stood, and walked around his desk. He opened the crate while the Voraxian held it, and I saw that I'd delivered a painting.

Just a painting, and I'd been worried about smuggling something like drugs or body parts or something.

The painting was an abstract art piece with hues from every color of the rainbow. Who knew that abstract art was popular everywhere? It was still ugly.

The Zyglar took the painting and placed it on a shelf behind his desk. He admired it for a moment before turning to me. "Your printer part is being delivered to your ship now," he said in accented English.

"How do I know?" I blurted.

He tapped his screen and then turned it so I could see the display. On it, some dock worker was wheeling out a square crate on a dolly. She deposited it in front of *Fetch*'s airlock.

"Satisfied?" he asked.

"I will be once I make sure it works," I said.

"It will. You have my word. A merchant wouldn't stay in business long if his goods failed."

"Cool. Then we're done here," I said.

"Any time you need more business, come my way. If you can't find me, ask for Qualixs. Everyone knows me around here."

I tilted my head in acknowledgement. "Thanks. See you around."

"Oh, and your body scan shows that you've got the cheapest Tardigrades out there."

"They're from my boss. She's a Zuddlian," I said.

"Ah. That makes sense. I'm surprised you even got Tardigrades. Your race must be exceptionally fragile for a Zuddlian to spend any cards on biological support."

I shrugged. "I'm getting by all right."

"Well, I have a special deal: softbotics upgrade for only two thousand cards that auto-translates the top forty major languages. I can make it the top sixty for just a few more cards. I have the same softbotics in here." He tapped his head. "And it never fails. I have over ten thousand languages, though. That's why I can speak yours."

"Thanks, but no thanks. I can't afford it."

"Well, you could get it with a payment plan."

I chortled. "No thanks. I've already got one contract to deal with. I don't want to owe a loan shark while I'm at it. No offense."

"None taken. But it's got to be a challenge reclaiming items when you can't speak. And I'd offer a fair interest rate."

I narrowed my gaze. "Why would you want to sell to me, anyway? I clearly don't have the cards."

He shrugged. "You're a reclamation agent. That means you're constantly traveling. That makes transporting goods more convenient."

I shook my head without even considering his offer. "I'll think about it." And then I left to take care of my "real" job.

Tzerina was the nearest station to Surlia, the planet on which the Undermarket was located. Evidently, the Calcar who'd paid for the repo ticket wanted to be as close to his daughter without being on the same planet. Gotta love family. Can't live with them, can't send Nebulan enforcers after them.

The Calcar I brought the necklace to was in Tzerina's poshest hotel. It was a nice break from alleys, nightclubs, and smelly docks. I took an elevator up to the client's room. I had to double check the symbols on each door with the symbols on Totty's instructions to make sure I found the right room. I tapped the small screen next to the door. After a moment, it lit up, and a Calcar's visage appeared. He said something in that guttural Calcarian language.

"Uh, I'm with Starshine Seizure Services." I still couldn't say my company name right without getting all tongue twisted.

The door clicked, and I entered a luxurious hotel room. Before me, a table set for one, bore a lavish spread of food. At least that's what I thought it was until I noticed the noodles were wriggling.

I tried not to pay attention and instead focused on the Calcar who had only a towel wrapped around his waist. Yep, Calcars still looked like orcs.

"Are you Koulra?" I asked.

He grunted something and then said, "Yes. You brought the pendant?"

I reached into my pocket and pulled it out.

He reached for it, and I yanked it back, pocketing it again. "I, uh, need visual confirmation that you received it and sent payment."

He stood there while I raised my tablet and held the screen in front of his face. My tablet beeped and then I read the screen. "It's processing now." I glanced at him. "You know, Tsara didn't want to give it up. She's not going to be happy with you."

He chortled. "That's because my mother wanted Tsara to have that pendant. It feels good to screw over the old hag one last time."

All right, so the Calcarian family unit was a bit more barbaric than the typical human family. My screen beeped again, and I saw that the transfer was approved, and that the Calcar had paid. A part of me hoped it hadn't. I grudgingly pulled out the necklace again. I saw Tinkerbell eye me and pound on the glass as I slowly handed her over.

"Argh." I couldn't do it. I slapped the necklace down, grabbed a thick silver knife from the dinner service, and slammed the hilt against the pendant. The glass cracked and then Tinkerbell escaped from the shattered pendant and zipped around the air.

"No!" The Calcar grabbed a humongous blaster rifle that must've been propped against the chair the entire time. He fired at Tinkerbell who easily zipped around his shots. He glared at me. "What have you done!"

He swung his rifle toward me. I had no time to go for my blaster, let alone duck. Just as he pulled the trigger, Tinkerbell attacked him.

Surprised to find myself still standing, I

laughed. "You saved me! Thanks, T," I said. A weirdly icy sensation washed through my left bicep, and I glanced down to find my arm was now lying on the floor. "Oh... crap," I said.

The pain hit me then, and with about four miracles, I managed to not keel over. Koulra fired again, and I somehow managed to run to the door, open it, and duck into the hallway. I propped myself against the door and gripped my left bicep (what was left of it, anyway). I thought I'd felt pain before, but anything before this was like a lightning bug compared to the white-hot lightning bolts shooting through my arm right then. It was like every nerve ending was screaming at me. The heat from the blaster must've cauterized the main artery, but I was still leaking a lot of blood. That's what happens when you have a giant hole in your body.

The hotel walls weren't blaster-proof because a shot burned through the wall near the door.

I stumbled down the hallway toward the elevator. The shooting continued which meant that Tinkerbell must've been holding her own against her slaver. When I reached the elevator, I was lucky I didn't have to figure out which button was up or down since the Calcar was on the top floor. I tapped the single button, groaning while I waited.

The door eventually opened, and a couple emerged. They looked relatively human except for pointy ears and bonier facial features. They reminded me of gaunt Vulcans. They'd been in the middle of a kiss until they saw me. Instead of helping, they gave me a wide berth as they hustled by with a look of disgust on their faces. They said something to me, and I was glad I didn't have a translator because I don't think they were being very nice.

I tripped entering the elevator and slammed against the back wall. The impact sent a tsunami of agony up through my arm, and I collapsed. Just before the door closed, a little Roomba bot rolled into the elevator, diligently cleaning up blood along the way. While the elevator descended, every time blood dripped from my arm, the bot would zip over, chirp, and clean before zipping back to the center to wait and watch with a single green-light.

When the elevator finally stopped, I grabbed the handrail and managed to drag myself to my feet. Wooziness nearly face-planted me, and I couldn't see clearly. Thankfully, the pain in my arm had become muted, though for all I knew, that meant I was dying. I didn't know of any-where I could go, so I made up my mind to get back to *Fetch* as quickly as I could. She'd know what to do about missing limbs (I hope).

Hotel patrons got out of my way as I stag-gered through the lobby. The Roomba bot chirped behind me. My vision was tunneling, and I wondered how much blood a guy could lose and still stay conscious.

I'd nearly made it to the door when a large, lumbering rectangular bot blocked my path. It said something to me, which I of course didn't understand, and I told it so.

"I am a medical response unit. I see you are damaged. Do you authorize me to repair you?"

My brain was getting squishy. "Yeah," I *think* I said.

"Authorization accepted. Repair commencing," the bot announced.

One side of the bot folded outward like a big ironing board and I collapsed face-forward onto it. I detachedly watched as the bot sprayed what looked like Vaseline across the entire wound, and the bleeding stopped. It was interesting to watch, but it injected me with something and then I don't remember anything else.

———

I came awake on a cold surface. My eyeballs felt like cotton and my tongue felt like sandpaper. I blinked until a big gray blur became shapes. I groaned and went to push myself up, only to hit my head on the floor when my left arm didn't support me. I glanced at it and squinted when I noticed that most of my arm was gone.

I'd really hoped that had all been a nightmare.

"Be careful, Frank. You're still under a significant dosage of painkillers and antibiotics," a gentle voice said.

"Fetch? Is that you?" I asked.

"Yes. The medical response unit delivered you here after it administered first aid. It deducted four hundred credits for treatment and supplies," she said.

"We had four hundred credits?" I asked.

"We did when Totty's payment for this ticket was deposited into your account. I should mention, Totty only paid half of the ticket since the client was killed in the transfer. The deduction is a penalty for losing a recurring client."

"He died?" I asked.

"According to Totty's note attached to the deposit slip," she replied.

"Huh. I guess Tinkerbell is tougher than she looks."

"By your response, is it safe to assume Tinkerbell is no longer in her prison?" she asked.

"I couldn't leave her like that. No one deserves to be a slave," I said as I gingerly poked at the skin an inch above where my arm had been blown clear off. The skin was pinkish and swollen but didn't hurt.

"Tinkerbell is an Anzu, a race considered far more dangerous and volatile than Calcars. The vicious Anzu nearly decimated the Calcarian home world two hundred years ago in an Anzurian frenzy. Tinkerbell has likely killed hundreds of Calcars in her lifetime."

Oh. "She looked so sweet."

"To quote an often-used phrase from your world: looks can be deceiving," Fetch said. "If the Anzu was released, I'm impressed you're still alive."

"She saved me. Mostly."

"The medical response unit said you were suffering from a blaster wound. Since Anzu do not use blasters, I assume the Calcar did not appreciate you releasing his captive."

"That's a safe assumption." I winced when I poked a spot that wasn't numb.

"You should be careful to not break the seal. Should you do that, you'll require an additional patch, which will cost you another four hundred cards which we don't have."

"On the bright side, we got a printer part finally," I said.

"We do. I had it loaded into the cargo hold. You will need to install it when you are able."

"How'd you load it?"

"I have drones."

"I didn't know that."

"You clearly don't know a lot about me."

"Touché," I said and closed my eyes.

"You should relocate to your cot. And your body needs rehydration."

"I'm too tired to move."

"No, you're too drugged and too weak. Move or else you'll die on my floor, and I don't want a Terran rotting through my floorboards."

I groaned. "Can't you carry me with your handy dandy drones?"

"You would not find them very comfortable," she said.

I groaned louder. "Fine." I managed to drag myself to an upright position and used the walls to help guide me to the ladder. I learned that climbing a ladder with only one hand is *hard*. I never realized how much I relied on using both arms until I had only one.

I was panting and had nearly blacked out by the time I reached level 1. I stumbled forward, sliding against the wall, until I reached the food station and began drinking water straight from the hose.

After several gulps, I said, "Hey, Fetch. Can I get another arm grown or something? There's got to be some fancy med tech around one of these stations that can do that sort of thing."

"Yes, but you can't afford it."

"Not even on a payment plan?"

"Not even close."

"Why can't space have universal healthcare?" I asked with as much depression as I was currently feeling.

"It does, but it's not cheap."

"Of course it isn't," I said drily as I plopped onto my cot.

"However, you may be able to afford an artificial arm. A Zyglar merchant would likely have access to that sort of thing."

"Which means I'll have to do more smuggling for one of the Q twins."

"The Q twins?"

"Quinixis and Qualixs."

"I don't think they're related," she said.

She said something else, but I was already drifting off to sleep.

————

I stretched out my bionic arm. I'd grown used to the whirring and clicking sounds. I hadn't grown used to it being twice the size of my old arm and having only a lobster claw for a hand. The arm only cost me everything I'd made on the latest ticket and then some. My cargo bay was filled with crates that I was delivering to some back-planet in a system called the Disputed Domain, which didn't sound ominous *at all*.

Here I was, financially (and bodily) farther behind than if I'd never taken the second repo ticket. I had to file a second extension to pay my GODly fines and was still waiting to hear back whether they'd granted an extension or if they'd planned to toss me on a prison world to rot.

There was one source of income, and I wasn't looking forward to what I'd have to do next. I sighed. "All right, Fetch. Reactivate comms." If I went much longer with my comms down, Totty might write me off for dead, which I hadn't decided if that would be a good thing or not.

"Comms are activated. You have two thousand three hundred and seventy-six unread messages from Totty," she said.

"Geez. Stalker much?"

"Zuddlians are known for their persistence. That's why you see so many in sales and management," she said. "Would you like me to read the messages to you?"

"Can you just give me the Cliff's Notes version? You know, a high-level summary?"

"I will do my best. I will also tone down her candor. Totty can be rather colorful when she's angry." A moment later, she said, "Totty does not believe that you had a comms issue, but she's not docking pay for it or adding years to your contract... this time. That covers all messages until final one where she assigns you the next ticket. I'm sending the full details of the ticket to your screen now. She says that she gave you two easy tickets to train you, and that you are now ready for a 'real' ticket."

I guffawed. "Those first two tickets were easy?"

"According to Totty, yes. She's assigned you to reclaim an abandoned ship."

I sat upright. "So there's no one to deal with. Just grab a ship and go?"

"Yes."

"That sounds like my kind of ticket." My interest was officially piqued.

"Totty ends the message saying that you will likely die."

I rolled my eyes. "Why did you have to go and say that?"

"I didn't. Totty said that."

I shrugged, which felt awkward since my left arm was so much heavier than my right arm. "I thought Totty wants her repo guys to live so she keeps earning money off us."

"Based on the ticket details, the payout for even a failed reclamation is so good, the off chance you survive is worth the likelihood of losing a new employee after the first couple of tickets."

I slumped back into my seat. Aliens are assholes. My boss is a dick, my ship is a sadist, and every freaking repo run ends up with someone trying to kill me.

Basically, being a space repo man sucks.

THE STORY CONTINUES...

Can you hit rock bottom in space?

Frank's a rookie space repo man struggling to get by in the cutthroat world of reclamation. As if dealing with creditors isn't hard enough, there are the ruthless repo agents like Krallix who swipes Frank's latest haul and turns his trusty ship, Fetch, into a floating scrap heap.

With his life on the line, Frank's survival depends on his somewhat questionable cleverness, a ship that's seen better days, and a bizarre alien slime he never should've laid hands on. Can Frank survive long enough to reclaim his haul?

Join Frank on this cosmic rollercoaster of mishaps, mayhem, and alien goo gone wild.

Get *Secondhand Starship* today!

ABOUT THE AUTHOR

Rachel Aukes is the award-winning author of forty novels, including *100 Days in Deadland*, which made *Suspense Magazine*'s Best of the Year list. When not writing, she can be found flying old airplanes over the Midwest countryside and catering to an exceptionally spoiled fifty-pound lapdog.

Join Rachel's spam-free newsletter to be the first to hear about new releases: www.rachelaukes. com/join

ACKNOWLEDGMENTS

With many thanks to Diane Bryant for making my stuff look good; to the Propellers for being the best damn writing group; to Brian for the hugs; to Ellie for the endless supply of doggie kisses; and to *you* for picking up this story and opening the galaxies within it.

Printed in Great Britain
by Amazon

39781286R00089